MW00916638

ANOTHER LAST CHANCE

Tristan Walker

ISBN: 9781097789474

First printing, February, 2018
10 9 8 7 6 5 4 3 2

Edited by Kevin Baldeosingh

Book layout by SC Designs

Where Imagination Comes To Life

Dimex Publishing
Trinidad and Tobago

ALSO BY TRISTAN WALKER

CREATIVE JUSTICE

Synopsis:
Jason Griffith is an ex-Navy SEAL with a vengeance. Returning to Trinidad after serving with the US special forces, Jason struggles to reclaim a place in society and, in an attempt to get quick cash, he reunites with old friends who are now car thieves. But things quickly go downhill. After the gang finds a large quantity of drugs in the trunk of a stolen vehicle, Jason is targeted by a notorious drug lord who goes on a killing spree and kidnaps Jason's only sister. Jason has twenty-four hours to find his former friends and return the drugs if he wants to see her alive again.

ACKNOWLEDGMENT

Thank you Mr. Kevin Baldeosingh, not only for the great work you have done in editing this book, but also for giving your best advice and knowledge during the process. Ms. Shrimati Charan, whose talent and expertise brought the book layout to life beyond my expectations. I still can't believe it. To my mother, brothers and sisters, for believing and being there for me from inception, and always being the first to read and comment on my craft. It was y'all enthusiasm that got me this far.

To my brothers and sisters who dedicate their days and nights serving our country, continue to do a great job and never be discouraged.

CHAPTER ONE

The alarm went off at 11:30 p.m., and Kevin jumped up. Beside him on the couch, Shantel stirred but did not awake. They had both fallen asleep on the couch watching a movie. Kevin pulled on a jersey and headed for the bedroom to start getting ready for the party. He had set the alarm a bit too late, since the guys had made plans to meet at midnight.

He moved from room to room, trying his best to remain quiet. But, as he was sitting on the bed pulling on his socks, Shantel appeared at the bedroom door. Her normally cheerful face was expressionless, which meant she was angry. He got up and started combing his hair. His back was towards her, but he saw her watching him, still expressionless, in the mirror.

"What now babe?" he said, turning.

"So, you mean to tell me you still going out, no matter how I feel about it?"

He shook his head.

"Babe, you being serious right now?"

"Yeah! Why not?" she said, raising her voice. "If you too blind to see that these fellas is not yuh friends, that is what I here for."

Kevin sat down on the edge of the bed and laced his shoes. Then he stood up and walked across the room and looked at himself in the mirror again. He liked the way he had coordinated the colors, with his red polo jersey, blue jeans and white sneakers. He contemplated whether to keep his gold chain inside or out and then tucked it under his jersey so he would draw less attention when he reached the club. He then turned and faced her again. She looked at him.

"Babe, why yuh always have to be worrying so much? I not even worried." He walked over to her. "What happen last time is in the past, we done get over that long time."

"Yeah but..."

"But nothing!" he said. "Stop worrying 'bout Biggs and them boys, let me worry about that." He was right up to her looking straight into her face, trying to convince her that everything was going to be okay. At least, if he said it enough, he too would also believe it.

"Babe, you not seeing the point," she said and attempted to walk away, but he held her hand.

"What is the point then, Shantel? You tell me."

She delayed a few seconds before answering. "You know this eh done here babe, and just the thought of something happening to you bothering me so much. Almost two weeks gone and everything going so good. I just don't understand why you feel you have to meet back with them tonight."

He released his grip and passed his hand across his face.

"Babe, I explain to you so much times that I only going because is Sean birthday lime and we did plan this way before anything did even happen. This is the last time I going out with them. I done tell Steve that already."

She held him in a gaze for a few seconds.

"Babe," Her voice was low. "I just have a feeling that something bad going to happen."

He gently lifted her chin and looked into her eyes.

"Shantel, babe, stop worrying about it please. You just being paranoid. Nothing going to happen, okay. I could guarantee you that."

A moment passed in silence.

"Yeah, okay, I hear you." She pulled away and shook her head and walked back into the living room, carefully lowering her body onto the couch.

"You know what. You go ahead and do yuh thing," she said. But her tone wasn't angry now, just sad. Kevin looked at her and he couldn't help but put himself in her position. He could understand what she was going through.

Two weeks ago, Steve had taken him along with their friends, Wendell, Sean and Marcus on what he claimed was a new drug pickup location. But, instead of collecting, he had stolen two kilos of drugs from a well-known drug pusher from Arima while Sean and Kevin remained in the car. They were both upset about what he had done and Kevin told Steve that he didn't want to be linked to him anymore. Sean had also decided to distance himself from the crew after the party tonight.

"Babe?" Kevin said.

Shantel ignored him.

"Baby…?" he said, but she continued looking at the frozen image on the TV. He began caressing her shoulders and then went around the couch and got down on his knees as if he was finally ready to propose. But then they were both distracted as the headlights from a car brightened the front window and loud gangsta music filled the night air.

No later than the car had stopped than the horn blew twice. The music and voices were sounding clearer; they both knew who it was.

Shantel gave him a long hard stare which was meant to be his final warning, but he simply smiled and got up and headed for the door, grabbing a Miami Heat jacket and Sean's gift on the way.

"Kevin…?" she said. "You forgetting something?" He hurried back, kissing her on her lips and then placing his hand gently on her stomach. He could feel the baby pushing against his hand.

Their eyes met again and he brushed his hand across her stomach.

"Daddy coming back in ah little while, okay honey." They both got another kiss, and he went smiling all the way to the door.

Outside was cold and dark although many of the neighbours' lights were on. And, as far as his eyes could see, there wasn't anyone walking in the streetlights. There were only a few cars speeding by as usual.

As he got closer to the car he could see smoke escaping through an open window and he smelled the weed even before he came close. But, thankfully Shantel hadn't come to the door.

Kevin pulled open the back door of the car and sat down and Marcus immediately stuck a half bottle of Hennessey into his hands. Kevin looked to the house and he could see Shantel standing at the door now.

"Goodnight Shantel!" Steve said, his voice lifting, as he used the steering wheel to pull his body forward and stick his head out of the window.

"Just bring my man back home safe, okay," she said.

Steve laughed. "Yeah, no problem. I hear you," he said and dropped his body back onto the seat. "You don't have nothing to worry about. We go bring Cinderella back home before midnight." He laughed and reversed onto the roadway, popping the horn as he sped off with screeching tires.

Kevin was stuck in the back with Marcus and Wendell and the half bottle of Hennessey, while Sean was in the front passenger seat, taking another pull of the weed. The secondhand smoke alone was enough to get everyone high since the other three windows were only slightly cracked.

"Hold this bro," Kevin said while coughing and fanning away as much of the weed smoke as possible. From the moment they'd began hanging out together Kevin had only smoked weed once, and that was probably the most intense five seconds of his life. With the first pull he felt as if he was being strangled by some sort of spiritual force. And when it was over, he was very thankful to be alive.

Sean turned slightly on his seat and took the gift and thanked him. He shook it a couple times, wondering what it could be and after getting no hints he placed it in the glove compartment to unwrap later.

They drove around for a couple of blocks and smoked out the weed before heading out to the night club in Tunapuna.

As usual there was a large crowd at the entrance. Steve had paid the booking fee so they were already on the list. Plus, the bouncer was one of Steve's good friends, so he'd always allow them to enter without being searched.

All of them except Kevin and Wendell were strapped with fully loaded automatic pistols, so moving through the crowd was the easiest part of maintaining their respect.

Kevin remained one step behind until they had gotten inside. At that point they were free to move around and mingle with whoever they chose, as long as they maintained a visual of each other throughout the night. That was their main rule when out in public. Another important rule was that they came together and left together, no matter what happened or how many girls they picked up.

There were a lot of women in the club and the DJ was playing a selection of the latest dancehall. Marcus ordered a bottle of Johnny Walker Blue, and they all began drinking shots straight, the bottle of expensive scotch standing at the centre of their table. They didn't look around, but they all saw which women were looking their way.

Within two hours or so Wendell had gotten so high that he'd started throwing money to some of the women who came to dance with them. This was his usual behavior when he drank, and one of the reasons he wasn't carrying a firearm tonight. One time he'd gotten so drunk that he pulled his firearm and fired three shots into the ceiling of a popular nightclub in Port-of-Spain. Thanks to another one of Steve's friends, that incident hadn't brought the police.

Kevin had reached his limit. He could usually hold his liquor, but it seemed as though the combination of secondhand smoke and scotch had made him higher faster. Now even the plain girls in the club were starting to look like America's next top models to him, and women who were obviously standing with their man seemed to be smiling and flirting with him. All this was a recipe for trouble, and he didn't want trouble. He made his way to the restroom and spent a few minutes washing his face, and by the time he went back to the dance floor things seemed normal again.

He made his way into a corner where he'd decided to spend the rest of the night, sipping on a glass of Cîroc and enjoying the view of a group of women who were wearing clothes designed to show their assets and dancing to match. A number of women came into his invisible cubicle and danced with him.

There was one young lady who did more than dance. She left an impression. She was by far one of the sexiest women there. She was dark-skinned, slim and had wild, curly hair. She wore a blue dress that ended just below her knees, and her four-inch heels complemented her dress.

She danced with him to her favorite songs and, when her songs weren't playing, she danced for him. He felt amazing. And he wanted to get to know her better.

Another one of her favorites came on and when it had finished and she was about to step away, he held her hand and pulled her closer to him. The place was dark, but between the disco flashes he'd gotten the chance to observe that her eyes were a sort of light brown. She didn't attempt to escape his stare or grip, welcoming his touch like the expensive drinks he'd sent to her before she'd come across.

"Problem…?" she said in a curious but friendly voice.

"Yeah…"

"What?" She was surprised by his answer.

"What you trying to do me?" he said.

She laughed and leaned closer to him. "What I trying to do?" She looked down at his hands. "You is the one who holding me hostage." Her eyes came back to his and she showed another one of those friendly smiles.

He couldn't help but smile back. "So, is like that?" he said.

"I don't know what you talking about," she said in a teasing voice. With her undivided attention he'd almost forgot that they were in a club. The DJ began making a promotional announcement and her smile came momentarily. She bit her lower lip in a seductive way and turned her head to the side. At that moment he slowly released her hand.

The DJ changed his style of music. Now she grinned mischievously at him.

"Question… You could dance to this, Mister…?"

"Jones… Kevin." Usually, he didn't give strange women his real name, but he felt unusually attracted to this girl. "And yes, I could, and I would love to."

She positioned her body closer to his and rested her hands on his shoulder. The chemistry felt more personal than the usual dance from a stranger. She quietly moved to the slow conscious melody and he followed. Soon enough she felt comfortable with his dancing and rested her head on his chest.

A few persons on the floor did the same while the others stood around enjoying their drinks and their conversation.

Throughout the beginning of the song the DJ encouraged more persons to join in but only a few couples obeyed.

Steve and Wendell were looking on from their table.

At the end of the second song, Kevin began to ask her where she was from, but she interrupted the question by tightening her grip. She made it obvious that she wanted to continue dancing in silence.

They danced to the final song and when it had ended she held his hand and led him to a table across the room where they sat down. Kevin shoulders became tensed and now he was nervous of her unknown intentions. Her actions suggested that she was looking for more than a dance or a casual conversation. But that was something he wasn't about to do because of his past experiences.

Kevin had been unfaithful to Shantel in the past, but he hadn't cheated on her since early last year when she had found out the heartbreaking news from the same young lady whom he was having an affair with. Because of that, they had separated for a few months and up until this day her parents hadn't found it in their hearts to forgive him for breaking their daughter's heart.

Kevin was looking everywhere in the party, except across his shoulder where she was sitting.

"You okay?" She wrapped her hands across his waist and gave him a gentle squeeze, finally getting his attention.

"Yeah, I good." He noticed that their glasses were almost empty. "You want another drink?"

She smiled and hesitated at first, and then told him yes. He left and returned a short moment after with a bottle of Cîroc. She looked impressed.

"I see you like to do it big." Her eyes were glued to the bottle of Cîroc.

"Nah, not really, I does hardly go anywhere, so I does just like to have a good time whenever I get that chance."

"Oh, okay. Cool."

He rested the bottle on the table and she filled both glasses and started drinking.

"So, what is yuh name?" he asked again.

"Christine."

"Okay." He leaned forward and stuck his hand across the table with a proud smile. "Nice to meet you Christine."

She returned the smiled and took his hand.

"Nice to meet you too, Kevin."

They both continued looking around the party and enjoying the music. She looked happy and was nodding her head to the rhythm of each song.

"So, where exactly you from?"

She looked at him and he could tell from her reaction that she was contemplating whether or not it would be wise for her to give out that type of information.

"What I mean is, you from around here?" He tried the question from another angle.

"Yeah, well. You could say that. I from right Macoya. What about you? Where you from?"

"Enterprise."

"Hmm, okay. And you come quite up here by yourself? So much party you like?" she said in a teasing voice.

"Nah," Kevin shook his head. "I come with them fellas over there." He pointed to the table where Steve and Sean were sitting. They were amongst four young women who were all dressed in tight, revealing clothing. They were all laughing and drinking and enjoying themselves. Wendell wasn't anywhere around. Kevin knew he must've mentioned something and left for the restroom or maybe to take a smoke, so he didn't put much thought into it. He turned back to Christine and noticed that she was looking over at their table in deep thoughts.

"What about you? Where yuh friends?"

Her attention came back slowly, and the glass went straight to her lips. The entire movement looked strange, as if something was bothering her. But, again, Kevin didn't think much of it. He was there to enjoy himself and he wasn't about to let the alcohol get to him.

"I don't have plenty friends, only one. She couldn't make it. Last minute plans with she man. You know how that is."

"Yeah, I know."

She refilled her glass. Kevin had barely drunk half of his.

"Talking about that." She quickly opened her purse and took out her cellphone. "I clean forget to message she and tell she I reach." She started typing out the message and Kevin waited. During that moment Wendell had returned and retrieved his seat at Steve's table where two of the ladies were dancing for them.

When Christine came off the phone they'd both continued talking about parties, her friend Cassandra and all her favorite drinks. She was drinking a lot faster than before and when asked about her transportation arrangements she explained that her cousin would be coming to pick her up.

During the latter part of their conversation she'd gone into her messages several times to update her friend that she was having fun. She'd even snapped a picture of both of them and forwarded it to her friend.

At 3:45 a.m. she received another message.

"Okay, that is him. He outside, in the car park," she said in a slurred voice and slid out of the seat. Kevin remained sitting and she'd placed her hands on the table and looked back at him.

"What happen? You not coming?" Her question was more like a plea for his company. She then stuck out her hand making it obvious.

They were already close to the door and Steve and the fellas were taking shots at the bar. Kevin thought about it and decided that he would sneak out and return without anyone noticing. Even though that was technically breaking their first rule, he felt somewhat responsible for her being so intoxicated. As he stood up she held him across the waist for support, making it much easier for him to leave without any hesitation.

The atmosphere outside was a lot different. It was quiet and cold with the full moon yellow in the dark sky. Kevin had given Christine his coat and the first gust of wind made him shiver, and he tried to hide it.

Only a few persons were outside, mostly smokers and cell phone abusers.

The bouncer flicked his cigarette and came back to the entrance. He raised his brow at Kevin as he passed by.

The further they walked, the more Kevin realized how drunk she actually was. She was literally leaning against him, making it difficult for him to walk straight.

"So, you had fun?" She looked up at him while talking. The strong scent of alcohol coming from her breath made him turn away. He kept his head straight.

"Yeah, it was good."

"Okay, cool, cause I could make it even better."

He looked at her with raised brows. The conversation was becoming inappropriate. Not only because of his intentions of remaining faithful, but because he knew that she was drunk and it was the alcohol talking. He had no idea what to say.

"How far he park?" he asked, changing the topic.

She studied him for a moment and then looked around. "He say he in the car park to the back." She was smiling and rubbing on his chest in a gentle, seductive way. "You want to have some fun?"

Kevin didn't need any time to think about it. She looked good, but he knew it wasn't worth it in the end. His intentions were simply to come and have a good time and the time they'd spent inside the club was more than he could've asked for.

"Nah, I good. Maybe some other time."

She stopped walking.

"What you mean, you good?" The smile was gone, and she had a concerned look on her face. There was something more to her eyes, something that only a conversation would reveal, but they had done enough talking for one night and time was against them.

"Hmm," she sighed. Her eyes becoming dreamy. "I like that. You know, exactly what you have home. More men should be like you. Or at least my man."

She started walking again and Kevin felt proud of the decision he'd made.

There were two parking lots and the one to the back of the club was a new addition with poor lighting and mostly deserted. Kevin thought it was strange that someone would go through the risk of parking there, especially if they were just here to pick up someone.

"Why he park so far, though?" Kevin asked while looking around. There wasn't anyone close by.

"I really don't know. I think he come with his girlfriend, so they must be want the privacy."

"Hmm," Kevin sighed, knowing that wasn't a good enough reason.

They entered the car park and he noticed her looking around and tip-toeing to see over the few cars. Something wasn't feeling right.

"What happen? You not seeing him?"

"No."

"What kind of car it is?"

She went into her purse and took out her phone. "I not sure, he does always borrow his friends' cars."

She started making the call. She was standing on her own and when the person answered, she told them that she was in the car park and hung up after their reply.

"He say he over here." She pointed in the direction

and started walking to the darkest area of the car park. Kevin kept behind hoping to see her enter the car so he could leave.

She walked up to a car and he noticed that she had gone closer to the trunk of the car instead of going in. She was looking at him with the same concerned look on her face and that was when he stopped. He knew something wasn't right and whether she'd decided to enter the car or not, he wasn't about to go any further.

Before he could ask anything, he heard footsteps running up behind him and he spun around.

"Wha… " he shouted out and felt something solid hit him across his back. He fell to the ground and began rolling from side to side, grimacing in pain. He received a few more blows across his arms and back.

"No, stop." He heard Christine say in a panicking voice and while struggling to catch his breath he heard more footsteps walking around him.

"You say you just wanted to talk to him," he heard her say in a crying voice.

"Yeah, well. We go talk just now," a man's voice said.

"Well, this wasn't part of the plan. I don't want anything to do with this, tell him he could keep the money."

Kevin looked to where Christine's voice was coming from and from a blurred vision he saw a man walking away and she got into a car and started the ignition and drove away. He could hardly make out anything else and turned away.

"Hmm… what we have here, boy?" another man's voice said. Kevin recognized the voice.

Biggs and five of his boys were standing over him.

They had surrounded him.

"What... you want?" Kevin said in a tough voice, although he was breathing heavily and still trying to fight the pain.

"You for real right now...? Nah, you can't be fucking serious," Biggs said, looking around at his boys. "This fool have to be kind of retarded." He walked closer to Kevin, standing in front of his face and then turned his back looking in the opposite direction. He looked frustrated. Kevin kept his eyes on all of them preparing for any sudden movements.

His eyes were away when he heard Biggs move and the instant he looked back at him the only thing he saw was the tip of his shoes and felt a hard kick to his face. His head jerked with the impact and it felt more painful than the rusty piece of iron that one of the fellas was holding in his hand.

Biggs' shoes had landed right below Kevin's left eye. Kevin put his hands on the spot and pressed against it while groaning in pain. He was now on his knees with his body in a crouched position as if he was begging for mercy. Biggs placed his foot on Kevin's shoulder and kicked on him causing him to tumble over and his body curled up on the ground. His hands were still covering his face.

"I want you dead. I want you, and all yuh friends dead. But don't worry. I going to accomplish that tonight. I going to cut you up in little pieces and send a message." Kevin was looking through his unprotected eye. His vision was getting dark, darker than the night.

Biggs looked at the other guys and walked away.

Kevin saw the look on their faces and he knew that he'd have to make his body as small as possible and hope that he wouldn't be beaten to death.

The guys started to close in on him and they began to kick, stomp and cuff him for what felt like five minutes. At one point he was even beaten on his back with the piece of iron.

When they had dealt their final kick and stomp they stood around in silence and he could see some of them smiling through a crease in his swollen eyes.

His entire body felt weak and sore and he lay there, certain he would not survive much longer.

They lifted him by his arms and feet and took him to a car where he was thrown onto the backseat. At that point he began to regret, not only leaving home or ambushing Biggs and his guys two weeks ago, but as far back as the day he'd met Marcus. He wished back then he could've seen this coming.

He vomited on the seat and realized he was too weak to move. Suddenly, he heard a commotion outside the car. The voices were getting closer and it sounded like Steve and Marcus.

A gunshot rang out and Kevin flinched and shoved himself off the seat to the floor of the car. He could hear Biggs's voice outside, shouting and instructing his boys to get into the car. The door opened with gunshots still firing from both sides and he felt their feet stomping on his head, shoulders and legs as they got into the car and it sped away.

One of the windows shattered and the pieces of glass fell onto his body. The car swerved around a corner and

Kevin could feel the breeze from outside coming into the car more freely.

As they covered a distance Biggs couldn't stop cursing. Kevin realized two of Biggs' men had gotten shot and had to be left behind. And someone from Kevin's crew had been shot too.

Kevin got some more stomps just for being in the position he was in, and when his groans become overbearing he was pulled up on to the seat to await his final moment.

They drove for a long time and came to a quiet area where trees and distant streetlights were the only things in sight. The car stopped, and Kevin knew it was the end of the line for him.

CHAPTER TWO

Kevin felt as if he was about to have a seizure. He was panting heavily and he leaned forward and placed his hands on his head as he began crying in his frustration. He couldn't see clearly, and his mouth was bruised and bloody so his pleas for freedom and forgiveness were soft spoken and ignored. He started to struggle, even as he continued begging for his life as he fought the blows from elbows and fists as they attempted to quiet him down.

"I said to shut the fuck up," the guy on his left said and landed another cuff to Kevin's jaw. Kevin held his face and leaned forward trying to mentally control the pain. Blood was draining from his mouth onto the floor of the car.

"Nothing better don't happen to John and tall man, or is fucking war. I swear," Biggs said in a loud voice.

"What about this one? You still carrying him back to the house?" the guy on the right said. Biggs looked back at them and shook his head.

"Right about now I don't really care about all that.

Just do whatever you have to do," Biggs said and turned back to the front.

It seemed as though Kevin's time had finally come. The car came to a stop in a dark spot and the guy to his left handed his pistol to Biggs and said he was going to the trunk for something bigger and better that would do much more damage. He got out and left the door open.

Kevin looked over his shoulder and realized that the guy on his right was busy loading an extended magazine. He then looked outside to the dark, descending hill. The guy said something to Biggs and then he heard the trunk close. At that moment Kevin pushed his body as hard as he could and dived out into the bushes and began rolling downhill. He immediately heard rapid and single shots cutting through the grass and trees around him. He kept his eyes shut tight and kept on pushing his body and doing anything he could possibly do to continue rolling. During that time it seemed as though the shooting would never stop.

He rolled into a shallow river, got to his feet quickly, and ran a few metres downstream and then across as shots hit the water. When he got to the other side he picked up the pace. The shooting stopped but he continued running full tilt. The further he got, the darker the forest got. Finally, he stumbled on a dirt track far away from the river. The moon was overhead. That was the first thing he noticed when he collapsed in exhaustion onto his back, taking large gasps of air. His wet clothes made him feel as if he was freezing and he was trembling and beginning to throb with pain all over.

After a few minutes Kevin got up and continued

moving again. It was not the way he would usually push himself, but he felt as though he was getting a second chance at life and he wasn't going to lose out on the opportunity.

About twenty minutes later he limped on to another dirt track. Some distance away, he could see a structure resembling a barn. It was very big, and he could see lights shining through two windows on the lower section.

He saw a dark silhouette walk across the room. It happened so fast that he wasn't sure if it were his eyes playing tricks on him. Whatever it was, he was about to find out.

He cautiously walked towards the building, remembering his earlier encounter. There were no trees in the area around the structure, only a few tree stumps. The grass was also cut. Kevin decided to scope out the area before attempting to call for help.

The side that he'd approached and the back was clear from any foreseeable danger and he slowly walked to the opposite side. He had to control his gasp of surprise.

There were two police cars and a large truck parked in a gravel area of the land. The only thought going through his mind, other than being dehydrated and weak, was that he was finally safe.

But then he walked back and peeped through one of the windows that he'd previously crept under and noticed something strange inside.

There were three rows of metal tables with lights hanging over them. There was also a closed door in the centre of the room. Kevin would have to go back around in order to see what was on the other side of the door.

He cautiously moved around the building to the other windows. Inside, the room looked identical to the last with the same iron tables and lighting overhead. The only difference was that there was a staircase leading to the top floor. Although he was confused by what he saw, he was satisfied that the police were there and he found that was a good enough reason to call for help.

He walked to the door and began shouting out to the officers or anyone inside. But nobody responded. Soon his throat began feeling sore and he felt a sharp pain moving up to his chest. The shouting was becoming too painful and he began banging on the door. That didn't work either. He was tired and knew he desperately needed to rest.

He walked across to the police vehicles and pulled on all the doors. They were all locked and there were no alarms to assist him in alerting the officers. Lucky for him the truck was left open. He gave it some thought and, although it was almost morning, he climbed in and made himself comfortable. But it seemed as though he had no sooner closed his eyes than he heard someone banging on the door and when he opened his eyes he saw a police officer standing outside the truck. He was startled and immediately sat up. He squinted against the glare of the morning sun.

The officer took a step back and gestured for him to open the door. Kevin rolled down the passenger window.

"Who is you?" the policeman said. He was a tall man dressed in blue and black tactical wear with two police emblems on the jacket. A machine gun was strapped across his chest and he held it at an angle that was easy for him to raise and shoot if he found it necessary. His finger was already on the trigger guard.

"My name is Marvin, sorry…" Kevin said.

The officer kicked the door to a close and lifted his gun, pointing it to Kevin's face.

"Don't fucking move. What happen to yuh face, and what you doing here?"

"Last night I did get lost and I try calling, but nobody didn't answer."

The officer was studying what was said and then began looking across his shoulders.

"Lost? And what happen to yuh face?"

Kevin knew he had no choice but to continue lying in order for his story to sound convincing. "I was hiking with some of my friends and things did get ah little out of hand."

The policeman was still looking around, but now in a more vigilant manner. "What? Hiking? And you decide that this was the best place to come and hide?"

"Well, yes sir. I see the police cars and it was kind of a quick decision. Again, ah really sorry. I didn't mean to cause any trouble."

Kevin heard a noise and when he looked over his shoulder he saw another officer walking towards them. He was similarly dressed and he was also carrying a machine gun and a pistol was in his leg holster. He looked as though he was born with a bad temper.

"What going on here?" he said.

"This little fucker get beat up, and lost, and decide that this was the best place to come and hide," the first policeman said. The other officer came up to the vehicle.

"Hmm, you get a good cut ass boy. They try to kill you or what?"

Kevin remained silent.

"Where you from?" the second officer said.

"Arima," Kevin replied.

The officers glanced at each other, then looked back at him.

"Arima?" The second policeman looked annoyed. "And you come quite up here to hike? You playing you is a fucking white boy or what?"

"No sir…" said Kevin.

"So is what then?" His voice got louder. It seemed as if Kevin's direct answers was pissing them off.

"Nothing," he said.

"Nothing?" The second policeman shook his head in exasperation.

"This look like ah fucking toy to you, boy?" He lifted the gun and pointed it at Kevin. Kevin pulled back as far as he could. "You feel this is ah fucking game or something?"

"N-no sir!" Kevin's voice was almost hoarse and he felt cramps in his stomach and his bladder was becoming weak.

"Come out the fucking truck!" The first policeman pulled the door open and Kevin almost fell on to the ground in front of them. The thought of dying filled his eyes with tears and he began pleading for his life between his heavy breathing. He heard one of the officers take a step back.

"Watch you now. Like ah little pussy. No wonder your partners them try to rape you." Kevin refused to look up at them. His hands and lower back was starting to give up on him, but he knew it was a pain he'd have to bear. They were quiet for a while and then he heard their footsteps circling him.

"So what you want to do with him?" one of the policemen said. He didn't hear what the other man replied. Kevin slowly placed his hands behind his head and interlocked his fingers. The pain was the only thing that eased.

They were both behind him now and he heard a fire-arm cock. A line of tears rolled down his cheeks.

"Please, officer," he sobbed. "Please. My girl preg-nant..." Neither one of them answered him.

"Hmm, boy. I really dunno," one of the policemen said. "He don't know anything and he done get a beating already. Killing him wouldn't make much sense..."

"Well, you have ah point there," said the second police officer. "And we go have to bury the body."

"Well, burying him is not the hard part. I just find it wouldn't make sense taking the trouble to kill this ass. He look like he could do anything?"

"Heh. When we expecting them, though?"

"Monday."

"So two days."

"Yeah, only two fucking days."

"And what about Samantha?"

"She somewhere inside."

"Well, it look like she have a patient to take care of."

"You sure you want to give she that stress?"

"Not really, but I killing too much people on this duty, I really didn't come here for that. I could let this one slide.

He wouldn't open he mouth about anything, anyway."

"Okay, fair is fair. Is your choice, so if you sure that is what you want to do, I don't have no problem with that." A few seconds passed and then Kevin heard the gun uncock and they were walking back to him. The second policeman came back to stand in front of him. Kevin had already made up his mind not to look them in their faces until they said he could go. The other officer stopped as though he was still thinking about what to do.

"Okay, get up." Kevin was shocked. He looked at them before attempting to stand up. His knees didn't work like they usually would.

"Listen, we was going to kill you, but I decide to let you live to see another day. Count yuh blessings," he said and looked at the other officer who was laughing.

"What you laughing about?" They were both smiling now.

"Let we cut it out now before the young man get a heart attack," he replied.

"Hmm..." He shook his head. "And I was now getting warmed up."

"Yeah, ah know. But, protect and serve with pride, right!"

"Yeah." He sucked his teeth and took a deep breath. "Unfortunately..."

"Let we go inside."

They walked at Kevin's pace and explained that things could get boring and they were only having fun. They apologized a couple times before explaining what they were doing.

The second officer, who was shorter and light-skinned, did most of the talking. He explained that they were part of the Narcotics unit and was monitoring the forested areas with the help of military personnel.

Afterwards, they helped him inside and led him pass the metal tables and went upstairs and told him to sit on the couch.

They went into another room and closed the door. Kevin looked around.

Straight ahead there was a large television and a dinner table with four straight-backed chairs. The flooring upstairs was wood and there was a rug on the ground and two more sofas. That was all the furniture in the room.

There were two open windows on the wall behind him and he could see the trees and the blue cloudless sky. The cool breeze came in momentarily. It felt very relaxing.

There were three closed doors on the eastern side of the room. The door where they'd entered at the top of the stairs remained open and that would be the fourth door upstairs.

Kevin rested his head and feet on the armrests and stared up to the galvanized roof while he waited for them to come out of the room. Once again his ability to focus felt restricted due to his aches and pains but somehow he managed to drift away.

"Marvin? Marvin, wake up!"

Kevin opened his eyes and lifted his head and saw both officers standing there in the company of a female officer. She was a round-faced woman, about forty years old, somewhat overweight but with strong-looking arms.

She was shorter than both of them and was wearing a navy blue police T-shirt and a black track pants. She began to visually examine him.

"Marvin, my name is Samantha. How you feeling?" His name took a while to register. He tried to sit up but she signaled him to stay put. She took a moment to observe his cuts and bruises, and then sat next to him.

"How you feeling?" she asked again

"N-not too bad," he said.

"Okay, good. I going to clean you up ah little, right?"

He nodded.

She physically examined him as gently as possible.

There was a silver basin filled with water on a coffee table next to them. A table that wasn't there when he had fallen asleep.

Both officers had vanished when she started to squeeze the cloth and brought it to his face. He flinched at first, but the pain quickly became numb to her gentle touch.

While cleaning him up Samantha asked Kevin some questions about how he had come there. It was easy to speak to her, so he found it natural to stick to his story of a camping trip gone sour.

At one point she had gotten emotional and stopped what she was doing to express her empathy. She then offered advice on how he should go about dealing with the situation. Kevin played along by asking several questions based on her advice.

When she was finished, she remained sitting there for a while longer. She told him that the dark-skinned officer was PC Puntin, and the light-skinned one was Corporal Richards. He told her of their approach and she said she was disappointed by their actions, though she promised to keep whatever he'd mentioned to her between them.

Samantha described their assignments, which were the same as mentioned by both Corporal Richards and Puntin. Kevin hesitated before asking about the metal tables, and she said they used them to take photos of the drugs before destroying them.

She got up and went into one of the rooms and returned with a change of clothes. Throughout their entire conversation he had been feeling dirty and ashamed of his appearance, so he was glad for the chance to freshen up. He went to sleep and, when he awoke, it was dark and frogs were singing their high chorus outside.

The night was long and cold. Kevin ate with Samantha and the other two officers at the table in silence and was then led back into the room where he had gotten dressed. There was an air bed on the floor and a makeshift rack on one of the walls with a few hangers. The only window within the room was difficult to close, so the temperature took some time to get used to.

Being in a strange environment made it difficult for him to fall asleep, while mosquitoes buzzed around the room and the night animals of the forest could be heard more loudly than he, an urban boy, had expected.

The morning came suddenly and, when he went out, he found that his three guardians—or jailers—seemed tense, hardly talking at all, even among themselves. Kevin was allowed to eat on the couch this time.

Samantha came after breakfast and informed him

that he would be getting a ride to the village during the early part of the afternoon.

He asked for a phone to call his family to tell them, that he was okay; she hesitated, then took out her mobile phone. But the call kept dropping.

"Reception not too good here. You will need to walk around till you get a signal," Samantha said. "You could try by them trees over there." She pointed. "That is where I does normally go."

Kevin nodded and went outside. That was the first time he had left the building since they had caught him.

He walked to the trees where she'd indicated the reception would be at its strongest. He dialed Shantel's number.

"Hello?" her voice sounded worried. He didn't answer at once as he noticed Corporal Richards was at the window upstairs, looking down at him. Kevin turned his back to him.

"Hello?" she said again, it was clear that she was already in her panic mode.

"Shantel?"

He heard a breath of relief coming from her end.

"Kevin… Babe, you alright?"

"Yeah, yeah babe, I okay."

She blew out a few short breaths as she started crying on the phone.

"Babe?"

She didn't answer.

"Baby?" he said again.

"Ye-ah…"

"What happen?"

"What you mean what happen? Why you don't like to listen to me? I did tell you to stay home, now look what happen."

Kevin was confused. What had she heard?

"What! What you talking about?"

"What you mean? I talking about the shooting, Kevin. Marcus dead and all of ah sudden you gone missing."

Kevin's heart was racing and he was forced to take some deep breaths. He wasn't sure if he'd heard right.

"What yuh mean, Marcus dead?"

"Kevin, is either you still not listening to me, or you playing. Now is not the time for that."

He was still in shock.

"Kevin… Kevin you there?"

"Yeah Shantel, I right here."

"What, you didn't know?"

"No…"

"Yeah, but it all over the news. Where you is now?"

He turned around. The corporal was gone. He couldn't see him anywhere. Kevin kept his eyes to the house just in case any of them decided to come out to get him.

"I don't know," he said.

"What, what you mean you don't know?"

"Is a long story." He shook his head. "I will explain everything when I see you."

"Okay…" Her voice was calm but the pain was still there. "When you coming home?"

"Tonight," he said, without being certain that it would be so. But he wanted to ease her mind. "Babe?"

"Yeah," she answered.

"What they say on the news?"

"What? Concerning last night?"

"Yeah, I wasn't close to a TV or radio."

"Well, the last thing I hear was, two people dead. Marcus, and some other person by the name of Timothy, I can't remember his last name, is either Jones or James or something like that. And Steve and another person in hospital, in critical condition."

Kevin took another deep breath. He remembered Biggs mentioning the names John and tall man, maybe John was the name Shantel couldn't remember. Putting four of them aside, it meant that there was a possibility that Sean and Wendell hadn't been harmed.

At that moment he noticed both Samantha and Puntin as they walked pass one on the windows upstairs, heading in the direction of the bedrooms.

"How you feeling?"

"Well," She breathed into the phone. "You had me worried, but I feeling better now."

"Okay, good to know that. And how we baby doing?" He kept his eyes on the window but they hadn't come out yet.

"She good, she kicking plenty. I feel she missing she daddy."

He smiled. "Okay, don't worry. I will see both of you soon."

"Yeah, next three months you mean," she laughed. She was speaking about the baby. He smiled. He was glad that her mood had changed for the better.

"Yeah," he said in a soft voice. Last night replayed in

his mind again. He remembered Shantel pleading with him to stay home and keep them company. He regretted that he hadn't listened.

"Well, babe, I will see you tonight, okay."

"Hmm, you gone already?"

"Yeah, I have to go. Is somebody phone I using."

"Okay, tonight then."

"Yeah."

"Love you, so much."

"I love you too, babe." He hung up and, immediately, cleared her number from the phone.

CHAPTER THREE

When Kevin went back into the building, he made sure to look around carefully.

There were cameras in every corner of the first room, and the adjoining room. His mood changed. He quietly walked up the wooden stairs.

This upstairs room had two cameras, facing the bedrooms. He sat down on the couch, thinking.

Kevin knew that since there were cameras it meant that there should be a screen where they could be monitored. He looked at the large television but there wasn't any device around it. But, why would they even need cameras to monitor what goes on in the storage room and especially upstairs where they are staying? The door opened and he turned and saw them coming out of the other room. He tried his best to remain calm.

Samantha said, "Marvin…? You okay? I didn't hear when you come back inside."

"Yeah, I now come up." The guys were watching him curiously, but they didn't say anything. "You got through with the call?"

"Oh, yeah, thanks." He handed the phone back to her.

"No problem," she said and started walking away and then stopped a few feet from where she was and turned back to him.

"Oh, I almost forget." Kevin lifted his head, giving her his attention again. "Corporal Richards will take you back to the village in a short while, okay?"

"Yeah, no problem." He tried to act as if it was really no problem. But because of the way they had acted when they had found him in the truck, he felt uncomfortable. If it was up to him, he'd rather volunteer to take himself, even if it meant walking through the forest.

They left to go downstairs to attend to the vehicles. After a few moments, Kevin got up and peered cautiously through the window. All three of them were outside. Quickly, he went into the other rooms—he wanted to find the monitor where the surveillance footage could be viewed.

After sneaking into the two other rooms and becoming satisfied that there wasn't any form of surveillance equipment there, he came back to the television in the main room to do a physical check.

It was just as he'd suspected. There was a processor unit, bolted onto the wall, hidden nicely behind the TV.

He went to the window and looked out again, making sure they were all out there before switching on the TV and the processor.

Twelve blocks of camera screens came up. He could see the iron tables of both rooms from four different angles, two cameras showed the bedroom doors and two focused on the outside of the building. On one of those cameras he could see Samantha and Puntin standing next to one of the police vehicles while the corporal searched through the trunk.

Kevin observed all the buttons and then pressed the playback button. He pushed the button a couple times to rewind the footage at its fastest speed, hoping that some activities would come up soon.

Finally, he began to see police officers and persons in casual wear. He slowed it down and, when he was satisfied that something was taking place, he sped it up again.

There were garbage bags and money and officers in khaki suits, leaving and entering on several occasions. Kevin didn't stop there. There were packages on the iron tables that were wrapped in plastic and the further he had gone back he saw both the men and women stripped naked. They were all wearing dust masks and were being guarded by officers in uniform with big guns.

Kevin jumped when he saw one of the naked men get shot once in the head and fall to the ground in front of everyone. Shockingly, they all continued working as if nothing had happened.

Kevin stopped and made checks outside the window again. The three of them were still there. The bonnet of the police vehicle was open and they were all standing around it. He examined the device and then pushed a button that ejected the memory card.

Getting it out was easier than he thought. He switched off the equipment and went back to the couch. At that moment his hands were beginning to sweat and couldn't stop shaking. He stuck the memory card in his pants pocket and lay down, hoping that he would stay awake.

His eyes opened when he heard footsteps coming up the stairs. He had almost fallen asleep, but he was thankful that he didn't allow himself to.

"You ready?" the corporal said, after realizing that he was awake. Kevin sat up and pretended to be stretching like the way he would after a relaxing nap.

"Yeah," he answered.

Puntin and Samantha were both standing behind the corporal looking on.

"Organize yuh clothes," the corporal said. "It wouldn't make any sense leaving them here." His eyes went to the time on his watch.

"Is four twenty-five. We leaving in the next half-an-hour."

Kevin went into the room where he'd slept and retrieved his clothes that was already bagged. When he returned everyone was downstairs again. He relaxed for an extra fifteen minutes before he started to make his way down the stairs.

"So that is what he tell you to do?" Kevin heard Samantha ask the corporal. He stopped where he was and began to listen.

"Yeah," the corporal answered.

"Hmm, well, better you than me," Puntin said.

"Yeah, but you tell him the fella don't know anything?"

"Yeah, but he say we can't be too sure and we can't afford to take that kind of risk."

"So, what you going to do?" she continued.

He laughed as if he was annoyed by her question.

"What the fuck you think ah going to do? Is either him or me. I don't know about him but I have a family to go home to."

"Well, I find he was kind of cool," she said, "but if that is what you have to do, don't waste the gas."

"Yeah, leave it there," Puntin said. "I'll organize and full the two vehicles sometime later."

Kevin felt as if he could faint. He could almost hear his heart pounding against his chest and he felt as if his body was becoming numb. He covered his mouth and slowed his breathing while trying not to panic. He looked up to the door and realized that he was already more than half way down the stairs. He had no idea whether he should run back up, or run pass them and through the door. Either way, he needed to get to the vehicle outside.

"Well, do yuh thing boss," he heard Puntin say. "Here, you could use my gun."

"No thanks, I have mine right there." He heard footsteps move across the room.

"Okay, well, I will go and cut off the engine," Samantha said. "Tell him I say buh-bye." He heard everyone moving around the room now.

Kevin slowly began to make his way back up the stairs while looking out below. The footsteps were getting closer and as much as he wanted to, he knew it would be difficult for him to move any faster without making noise.

There were only four more steps in front of him, and he could see the shadow approaching the stairs. He held his breath as he experienced fear from his stomach to the back of his head.

Only two more steps to go. Kevin saw the machine gun in the corporal's hands, and immediately moved.

"Aye! Fuck!" the corporal shouted when he spotted him. Kevin leaped into the room and slammed the door shut. He could hear the corporal running up the stairs, who began turning the door knob and kicking on the door.

Kevin grabbed a chair from the dinner table and launched it through the window. There was a galvanized landing just outside the window and at least a ten feet fall before hitting the ground where there was now broken glass and the broken chair.

The police car was at least forty or fifty feet away. Kevin looked towards the door when he realized the kicking had stopped. Shots were fired at the door, but half of his body was already out of the window within the first shot. He jumped onto the galvanized shed, fell off and landed with a painful roll. He looked up and saw Samantha a few feet away. She was reaching for her firearm. He got up and tackled her, sending her flat on her back, then leaped to his feet and continued towards the police vehicle. Bullets whizzed past him from the upstairs window.

Kevin dived parallel to the vehicle, opened the door and got in, shielding himself beneath the dashboard. Bullets were hitting all about the vehicle, shattering the glass and penetrating the hood and bonnet.

Kevin remained hidden a while longer, hoping the corporal would have to reload soon, but when the automatic firing had stopped he could hear single shots being fired from a closer distance. He couldn't stay there. He had to move if he wanted to stay alive.

He remained in an awkward lying position and mashed on the gas pedal and steered the vehicle while peeping through a crease of the open door. His view was obstructed with every swing of the door, but he had no intentions of slowing down.

Luckily the car raised a cloud of dust. He entered a dirt track as the bullets continued hitting the back and around the car.

When he had gotten at a further distance and the gunshots were sounding faint he came up and took control of his driving.

The car's windshield was shattered, and the windows and doors seemed riddled with bullets. It even smelled of exhaust fumes and gunpowder. Kevin was in so much pain from the fall that he couldn't tell if he'd been hit. Nevertheless, he was thankful to be alive.

There were high bushes and trees on both sides of the track and the sun was setting across his shoulder, between the trees. No streetlights or houses were within his view and the place was getting dark fast. He knew that soon the corporal and probably other officers would be after him. There was a wireless set in the vehicle and he tried every button before getting it to come on. The first thing he heard was a police unit calling for assistance to set up a roadblock at a junction whose name he didn't recognize. He had no idea where he was or how far the roadblock would be. But he knew that it meant he would have to abandon the vehicle and get off the road soon.

The sun had disappeared, and he continued following

the road with only one dim headlight. A short distance later he approached streetlights and had entered a village with lots of wooden houses. Nobody was outside. The place looked very quiet and peaceful. He turned a knob on the wireless set and scanned through the transmission frequencies while listening for anything in connection with the search for a man who had stolen a police vehicle. On one frequency he heard an officer confirm that the viper was at least ten minutes away. He kept it there. A few seconds later another officer confirmed that the K9 unit was also on their way. Kevin reminded himself of the stories he had heard about the capability of the police tracker dogs. He wasn't about to take any chances. He would have to get rid of the vehicle sooner than he thought.

"The vehicle with Sergeant Jacob, communicate with WT43!" he heard someone say over the wireless.

"Roger, Sergeant Jacob standing by, send!"

"Roger sir, viper is overhead waiting for your instructions."

Kevin rubbed his palms on his pants in an effort to keep them from getting moist. His nervousness and panic attack was creeping up again. He'd have to abandon the vehicle now. He couldn't risk staying in it any longer. He stopped near the edge of a hill and searched for anything useful. He found a pistol in the glove compartment with eleven rounds. He took it and stuck it in his waist, before pushing the car off the hill. As the wheels came off the road it began accumulating speed with ease, mowing down small bushes as it trundled downhill, leaving a trail behind. There wasn't any way for Kevin to be informed now, since the wireless set was gone with the vehicle. But one thing he knew for sure was that he had to keep moving. He began trotting towards the village.

In the first yard he came to, he saw a pickaxe next to a dirt trench and he took it up while running. He could hear a helicopter approaching. Some metres down there was a dark wooden house that looked vacant. Kevin entered the yard and went into the small veranda. He hooked the pickaxe through the padlock and levered the clasp out of the wooden door. He went inside and closed the door and quietly searched through the rooms of the house. There wasn't anyone inside. He went into the bathroom where he secured the memory card and firearm and stripped naked, turning on the water and rubbing soap all over his skin. He put his clothes in a corner of the bathroom, then sat in silence praying that he would escape the officers searching for him.

CHAPTER FOUR

Many hours later, Kevin was surprised the police hadn't discovered him. He had seen the blue flashing lights outside through the spaces in the wooden planks, and even heard footsteps and voices as the officers came into the yard. But there weren't any dogs and the helicopter remained circling the area long after the officers had walked away.

Kevin came out of the bathroom shortly after the officers had left. He was cold and trembling. He went into one of the bedroom where he dried up and found some clothes that were two sizes larger than what he wore. He threw them on and started looking around. He was still confused as to where he was, so he searched through the wardrobe and drawers for anything with an address. But there wasn't anything in either one of the two bedrooms. He left the room and went into the kitchen.

There was an open envelope stuck to the refrigerator with a magnet souvenir from Ft. Lauderdale. There were other souvenirs that represented parts of the Caribbean and also colourful magnetic letters that formed the words, "JESUS IS LOVE." He moved the envelope and began to examine it. He saw the name Emanuel Charles and an address reading Stone Street, Upper Village, Brasso Seco.

Kevin was shocked. He stood there for a while trying to come to terms with the address he was looking at. He stuck the envelope back onto the refrigerator and looked away. He was a long way from home, and he had no money nor the slightest clue as to how to get out of the village.

He walked back into the bedroom in a desperate search for cash or anything with a resale value.

While searching he noticed a jewellery box inside a cabinet in one of the rooms. Inside the box there was a gold chain and two gold rings. He threw them out into his palm and knew right away that they weighed somewhere between twenty and thirty grams. He played with the weight for a while, trying to calculate a street value and whether or not he'd find a potential buyer in such short time. He pushed away the thought and stuck everything into his pocket and continued looking around.

It was almost 4 a.m. and Kevin had no intentions of sleeping. He wasn't in favour of being caught off-guard by Mr. Charles or the police, so he stayed up on the couch for the remainder of the night and left before sunrise and began walking quickly down the road. Outside the sky was a dark grey and, although there wasn't any wind Kevin felt his body shiver every time he slowed his pace. The trees and grass were covered with dew, and a speeding car would pass by every ten or fifteen minutes.

Kevin continued walking with caution, carefully

observing everything that approached. He could hear insects and birds chirping, and the roosters were crowing. He had already been walking for nearly an hour and he had no idea if he was going in the right direction.

The sky was getting lighter now, changing to pale blue. On his left he could see a shop on the top of a hill. An elderly man had just opened up. Kevin saw when he'd propped the wooden door with a piece of stick and carried a stack of newspapers back inside. Kevin turned and walked in that direction.

His legs were starting to cramp, but he'd managed to get to the top. He stepped inside. The shopkeeper looked to be in his mid-seventies. His head was bald and he had a mixture of grey and black facial hair, and his eyes were dark and puffy.

"Morning, you alright?" the man asked, looking concerned.

"Yeah," Kevin said, "just had a little accident last night."

The man said nothing, so Kevin continued: "I need a lil favour, though."

"It ah little too early to be asking for favours. You don't think so?" said the man. It could have been a joke, but his face was impassive.

Kevin half-smiled, regardless. "Yeah, but I have to go to the doctor. So, as much as I don't normally do these kind of things. I have to ask."

The man sighed. "What you need?"

Kevin walked closer to the wire mesh that separated them, exaggerating the effort it took for him to move, although he didn't have to exaggerate much.

"Take yuh time, I here for the day," the man said.

"I staying right by my cousin up the road, but he going through some personal problems." Kevin unhooked the chain that he'd placed around his neck and then took off the two rings from on his fingers.

"How much you will give me for these?" He rested them on the counter beneath the mesh. "I don't want to sell them, just pawn them until ah get some money next week. They have sentimental value."

The man didn't pick up the jewellery until he heard about their sentimental value.

"Where you get them from?" He was inspecting them against the light.

"It was from my mother, she died two years ago, is all I have to remember she. Well, beside some old pictures. God rest she soul."

"Hmm." He was doing some thinking. His eyes moved between Kevin and the chain for a minute.

"Nah, I good," he said and rested it back on the counter. "I don't really like to make these kind of transactions."

Kevin was upset. The only thing on his mind was getting out of the village, no matter the consequences. He took a step back and examined his surroundings. The sun was beginning to peek out but there wasn't anyone outside this early. Kevin noticed that the gate that separated them was opened and the man remained standing across the counter, anxiously waiting for him to pick up his stuff and leave the shop.

Kevin began walking towards the gate. The man did the same.

"I don't want no trouble," the man said while quickening his pace.

"Me either." Kevin answered and kicked open the gate before the man could reach the latch.

Kevin was now inside the shop. He held onto the old man's arm, roughly guiding him back to the counter.

"Just give me what I want and everything would be alright," Kevin said and gestured for him to retrieve the money from the drawer. Kevin took up the jewellery and stuck it back into his pocket. The man took out two hundred-dollar notes and handed it to Kevin. There were more hundreds, tens and twenties in the drawer. The sight of it got Kevin angry. He pushed the man across the room and snatched up all the money besides the fives and single dollars notes and ran out of the shop.

He made his way about half mile down the street and hid himself behind an old bus shed.

The sun was now out, giving him a better look at the place.

There were hardly any cars on the road, but within twenty minutes more people showed up and soon after all of them had gotten into a bus. The ride was long and everyone came out at the bus terminus in Arima. From there it had taken him three taxis and a fifteen minutes walk before he was outside his Enterprise apartment.

He walked around the building and made sure it was safe before calling out to Shantel. She answered after his third call and came to the door. She was still wearing her night gown.

"What the fuck, Kevin! What happen to yuh face?" She stretched out her hands to touch the scars, but he stopped her short.

"Is small thing," he said, and made his way inside. She closed the door behind him.

He went to the couch and she went sitting next to him.

"You didn't tell me that you get beat up so bad!"

"No, and this is exactly why. You does overreact for every little thing."

Her expression changed. "This is ah little thing?" She grabbed his cheeks, and he flinched.

"What you trying to do? Finish what they start?"

"You see yuh face, and you saying is nothing serious. What? They brainwash you, too?"

"No, you crazy," he said, before realizing that it wasn't an actual question. "And where you get them clothes?"

"Is a long story." He walked into the bedroom and started to undress.

His arms and lower back pained the most, and when the jersey was half-way off, he noticed her standing at the door. As usual, she wasn't giving up that easy. He also saw that parts of his chest and stomach were discoloured. This was the first time he'd noticed it.

"Oh my gosh!" She saw it too. She covered her mouth and walked over to him. "Look at yuh skin, babe." She gently touched the bruised spot. He winced, but allowed her to continue. He knew she was only expressing her concern. He had put her through so much that he couldn't avoid that.

"Babe," he finally held her hands. She looked as if she was about to break down and cry. Her eyes were filling up with tears and a single teardrop trickled down her cheeks.

"Look at me." She lifted her head and her eyes met with his. "I will be all right, I promise."

She shook her head at the situation and held him cautiously, so as not to cause him any pain.

He was thankful to be in her arms again. He held onto her and they stood there in each other's arms for a moment. He could hear her crying.

"Babe?" she said.

"Yeah," he answered as they loosened their grip a little. She looked up into his eyes again.

"Would you promise me?" She paused. He waited for her to finish. "That you wouldn't look for any kind of revenge from this."

He gave it a quick thought. Not the promise, but the relief she was expecting to get out of it. Although not agreeing with her would seem kind of harsh at the moment. Because of all the second chances he had gotten, he knew he could use it as a warning and easily make the promise not to avenge Marcus's death. But he had run into something much bigger with the police and their drug house. And as much as he would want to end it at this instance, it wouldn't. And, he wasn't about to fill her in on those details just yet. It could jeopardize his family's safety and he wouldn't allow that.

But Shantel wasn't just waiting for the answer. He looked down at her and he could see that she was trying to get the truth from within his eyes.

"Yeah babe, I promise." He removed his hands. "I went through plenty, and I not going to risk it again," he said.

She believed him.

"Thanks, cause I can't continue living like this."

He gave it a moment to settle in. "Yeah, I know. Sorry, and thanks for being here for me."

They kissed, and she sat on the bed while he finished undressing and went into the shower. After getting dressed he began filling her in with the details which ended on the couch forty-five minutes later.

In his explanation, he'd replaced the woman in the blue dress with a long-time friend who wasn't at all responsible for the altercation. He also kept the police as the ones who had taken care of him and later took him out of the village like they had promised.

She had her moments during his explanation, but her emotions were at its highest when he described the way he'd barely escape from Biggs and his boys with shots firing all around him.

When he was finished, her hands were covering her mouth in shock.

"Hmm, babe," she said. "You really went through a lot boy. Thank God you here now."

"Yeah, for real."

They sat in silence. He was still a bit shaken up and the sounds of the vehicles passing outside had him nervous, since he was certain that the police officers weren't going to give up their search for him just yet.

"What was the latest on the news?" he said, breaking their silence.

"Well, nothing change in terms of the investigations. They still searching for the suspects. And, up until last night they didn't have any further information."

"Okay."

"Yeah, the cameras around the club wasn't working either, so they calling on eyewitnesses from the public to come forward. You know how that going to end up."

"Yeah."

They both knew all too well that witnesses never come forward after a shooting. They were always fearful for their lives. And the way crime had risen within the last couple years, no one could blame them.

"You going and report it to the police?" she asked.

"Yeah, most likely," he lied. After what had happened last night, going anywhere close to a police station was the furthest thing from his mind. He would have to wait until things cool down and then give it some serious thought.

"You hear anything concerning Steve and the rest of them?" he said, getting back her attention.

"Yeah. Steve still in hospital and Sean called last night. He say to tell you he in south, and to call him as soon as you get a chance."

"How he sounding?"

"Normal, he didn't talk much, but he leave a number that you could get him on. I put it under the phone book."

Kevin looked to the kitchen counter where the phone book was resting next to the house phone. It was where they'd normally leave any important message for the other person if they were about to leave the apartment.

"Okay, I would call him a little later. What about Wendell? You hear from him?"

"No, I eh hear anything from Wendell since."

"Oh, okay." Kevin was a bit disappointed. Besides

Steve, Wendell also lived in Enterprise and even if he couldn't call to check up on him, at least he could've come across to find out if everything was okay. Kevin dismissed the thought, choosing to enjoy the moment.

Shantel was quiet again. He could tell that she was still trying to come to terms with everything that he'd just told her.

He held her around the waist and brought her closer to him.

"Babe, you don't have anything to worry about, okay," he said, hoping that his words would comfort her mind. She looked straight into his eyes.

"Yeah, I know. I just wish none of this madness did ever happen in the first place."

"Yeah, me too."

They remained there for a while and then he stood up. He was very tired since he hadn't slept for the night and his eyes were taking him in and out of darkness.

"I feeling weak," he said.

Shantel nodded. "Go and rest."

Kevin went into the bedroom and threw himself on the bed and slept for most of the day. Shantel stayed in the living room, relaxing on the couch.

During the night he woke up feeling a lot better. Shantel was asleep beside him. He got up quietly and secured the memory card and the other items and then went to the phone book to retrieve the contact number that Sean had given to Shantel. The number looked familiar, but he couldn't place who it belonged to. He thought about how the conversation should go and then picked up the phone and dialed the number. A woman answered on the fourth ring. He recognized her voice.

"Who is this, Keisha?"

There was a short pause before the person answered.

"Who is this? And who you trying to reach?"

"Keisha, is Kevin. Steve leave this number for me to call him. He around?"

"Hmm, Kevin. That is not the way to answer a phone eh. Yeah, he right in the next room, hold on."

Keisha was Sean's eldest cousin. She was a registered nurse from a hospital in south and she lived in Rio Claro with her mother and his other cousins. Kevin had been there a few times helping out with some renovations.

He heard noise coming from a radio or TV and then heard persons laughing and talking before it was quiet again.

"Sean," he heard her say. "Kevin on the phone," she said in a lower voice and Sean answered a few seconds after.

"Kevin, what going on with you boy? Shantel tell me you suppose to reach home since last night."

"Yeah, I did tell she that but last night was crazy."

"What you mean?" Kevin could hear the concern in his voice. He walked to the bedroom to make sure Shantel was still asleep and then walked to the furthest part of the kitchen where he'd still see her. He lowered his voice.

"Boy I get tie up with some police."

"What you mean you get tie up?"

"I can't tell you everything now, cause I still trying to figure it out, but after that whole scene with Biggs I end up running into some police who in to some illegal shit."

Sean was quiet but Kevin could hear him breathing into the phone so he knew he was still there.

"What kind of illegal stuff we talking about here?"

"Boy, cocaine or some other kind of white drugs. I see a video with the people processing it and the police even shoot and kill somebody in that video."

"You serious?"

"Yes boy. I telling you exactly what I see with my own two eyes."

"Hmm." Sean paused as if he needed a moment to think. "And where the video now?" he asked. Kevin thought about whether or not to mention it over the phone and realized that he had already said too much. He had seen movies where police would trace and monitor phone conversations, but he'd never heard it being done in Trinidad. Regardless of their technology, he would rather discuss everything else when they met in person.

"I have it somewhere. We go talk nah." Sean understood the code. "What you doing in south anyway?"

"Boy, I pick up one on my hand."

"What?"

Kevin noticed Shantel turning on the bed. He placed the phone to his chest while observing her and when she found a comfortable position she was normal again.

"It bad?"

"Nah. It went straight through, but it didn't hit any bone, otherwise I would've have to be right next to Steve."

Kevin remained quiet hoping that Sean would get to the part where he'd decided to go to his cousins.

"After the shooting I notice Steve, Marcus and two other persons on the ground. My hand was bleeding but it wasn't hurting that much, so I manage to take up their guns and I hide in the bush and call my cousin who living Chaguanas to come and pick me up."

"So you take up everybody gun?"

"No, just Marcus and Steve own. I wasn't studying all that. But, if the police get their guns that would be good, because it would look like ah ambush."

"Oh, okay." Kevin didn't know what to think or what else to say. He was shaken up on hearing Sean relive the experience. He could feel a tightness moving up his spine to the back of his head.

"Okay, so what you saying? You have the guns with you now?"

"No. I leave them in the bush, but don't worry I wipe off any prints so even if the police find it, it wouldn't be useful."

Kevin's mind went on Marcus again and he was thinking about the pain he must've gone through before he had died.

"So Marcus was dead all that time?"

"No. He and Steve was breathing when I was picking up the guns. Steve wanted to come with me but his foot was damaged bad. I was next to Marcus and he ask me how it was looking and I tell him everything would be okay. While I was talking to him I see people coming and that was when I went in the bush. I would've stayed with them, but remember I eh clear up that warrant thing yet."

It was only then that Kevin remembered Sean had a warrant out for not attending court for procession of marijuana for the purpose of trafficking. He had been transporting it for Steve and it was the first and last time he had ever done something like that.

"Imagine getting shot and yuh best friend dying on yuh birthday." Sean said. "Some life eh?"

Kevin understood how Sean would be feeling. He was not shot but he compared being shot to everything that he'd been through and he could feel the pain of losing a best friend.

"It real hard, I know."

"Yeah."

Kevin gave Sean a moment to overcome his emotions. He listened to his breathing and when the silence was becoming lengthy he asked when he was planning to come back home.

"I not sure. Once nothing eh come out of the shooting I would come back down. Maybe next week or the week after."

"Okay, cool."

"Yeah. You call Wendell?" Sean asked.

"I try calling him earlier but he didn't answer. I will try back later tonight or in the morning."

"Okay. I would continue calling him from this end too. Once I get him I will let you know."

"Okay, good."

"Later, be safe up there. And don't forget to watch yuh back."

"Yeah, later." Kevin waited for him to hang up and he kept the phone in his hand recapping the emotional part of the conversation.

The following morning he prepared breakfast before waking Shantel up. He had done some thinking and asked her to spend some time at her parents' place until everything cleared up. She was a bit skeptical at first but after his, "keeping his family safe" speech, she agreed.

When they had finished their breakfast he helped her get her stuff together and then took her to her parents' house in Gasparillo. He remained in the car to avoid any questions that they would surely ask if they saw his battered face.

Her parents were more than excited to see her, so a reason for her surprise visit was the least of their worries.

Kevin got back home just after five and without any second thoughts he headed straight for the couch to rest his eyes.

CHAPTER FIVE

It was seven o'clock and the evening news had just started. Kevin sat up and turned up the volume on the TV. His alarm had gone off twice within the last fifteen minutes; he had put the clock on this setting to ensure he didn't miss any news updates on the nightclub shooting.

The house was in darkness as he hoped to mislead his neighbours into thinking that no one was at home.

"Good evening Trinidad and Tobago I am Jennifer Corbett-Smith and I'll be bringing you the seven o'clock news." Ms. Smith was pretty and fashionable and looked like she had never met the kind of young man who made the headlines she read out every night. "Two young men were shot and killed in separate incidents in Port-of-Spain and central Trinidad within the early hours of the morning. Public servants continue their rally for better working conditions. And the government is said to be looking into new ways to prevent road traffic accidents," she continued.

Kevin sat through the entire broadcast, including

the weather report, but there wasn't anything about the shooting or the incident that had taken place in Brasso Seco. He got up and attempted to call Wendell again. He had been trying him every hour for the past few hours, but all his calls went unanswered. He took a shower, put on a T-shirt and sweat pants and left the house through the back door, hoping that he would catch Wendell at home or his mother would help by at least giving some information about his whereabouts.

At 8:45 p.m. Kevin was walking through Wendell's neighbourhood. It was a very lively area of Enterprise, with a lot of young idle men liming on the street corners. At certain corners a strong scent of weed filled the air and on other corners there were men gambling under the streetlights and drinking alcohol. Had a stranger been walking by, some of these young men would have robbed him without hesitation, but Kevin was known to them, at least by face.

He made his way through a dark alley and arrived at Wendell's house. The lights were on and he also recognized the light coming from the television screen, which was playing loudly. He removed the chain and entered the yard like he usually did and went to the front door where he knocked a few times and waited. After one minute had passed with no response, he knocked again, but much harder.

The television was muted.

"Who is that?" a voice said. It sounded like Wendell's younger sister.

"Kevin!" he answered.

"Kevin? Hold on."

She came to the door with a surprised look on her face, which changed to concern as she saw his bruised and swollen face. "Kevin!" She hugged him for a brief moment and then pulled him inside. "You alright? How you feeling?"

"Hey, Karen. Yeah… well, I feeling a lot better than I was feeling a few days ago. I know you hear what went on, so I just trying to cope with everything."

"Yeah, I know. I could imagine what you went through. It so good to see you, though."

"Yeah, thanks. You too. Wendell home? I try calling him whole day but I only getting voice mail."

"Yeah, he in he room. He now finish bathing."

"Okay…"

"I will tell him you here."

Karen went to the back and he could hear her call out to Wendell. She came back and said that he would be coming in a short while.

Their mother and brother had left for church, so Karen and Wendell were the only two at home. She tried asking him about what had taken place but he told her that he was still a bit shaken up and would rather not talk about it.

A short while after Wendell came out of his room and signaled Kevin. Kevin got up and they went back into the bedroom and closed the door. Wendell was observing Kevin's bruises. Wendell, on the other hand, had no visible marks or wounds. Kevin found this strange, but he didn't say anything.

"What going on?" Wendell said.

"Nothing much, what going on with you?"

"Well, I just here, holding on."

"Okay, I trying to call you whole day."

"I lose my phone that same night in the scuffle. Might go and buy another one sometime tomorrow." He walked to his bed and sat down.

"Okay." Kevin watched Wendell intently, and Wendell shifted uncomfortably under his gaze.

"What?" he said.

"You look okay," said Kevin.

Wendell nodded. "Yeah."

"You didn't end up in the fight?"

"Sort of, but not entirely." He was looking straight at Kevin. "Remember, I didn't have nothing on me. I wasn't going to play no hero."

"So, what went on then?"

"I do what anybody else woulda do. Run."

Kevin shook his head. "I could imagine," he said dryly.

"If it was you, you would've done the same thing."

"I highly doubt it."

Wendell laughed. "Yeah, well knowing the hero that you is. If it was you, you wouldn't be here today. So count yuh blessings."

"Okay pardner. I hear you."

"I hope so."

Dogs suddenly started barking outside; Kevin looked out the window. Wendell's neighbour had just pulled up in his car and was opening his gate to drive in. Kevin closed the curtains and turned back to Wendell.

"You know," Kevin said. "The funny thing is how we can't see into the future. Otherwise, none of this would've happened."

"Well don't beat up yourself because nobody could. Plus, this wasn't your fault. If we didn't take them stuff from Biggs, none of this would've happen."

Kevin thought about it.

"Yeah, true. Is like one thing would keep leading to another until we go right back to the day we met."

Wendell shook his head and laughed.

"Yeah, you have a point there."

Kevin was looking straight at Wendell but his mind was reliving his memories of the past. He couldn't help but think of how good his life would've been if he hadn't met either one of them.

An awkward silence fell between them. After a minute, Wendell stood up.

"Look, Kevin, I really sorry for whatever you went through."

"Okay."

"I could see it was rough. But, with all that happen it good to know that you alive and that is something you should be thankful for."

"Yeah, I know." Kevin cleared his throat. "I actually feeling like I living another life."

"Yeah, me too."

Kevin looked at him with a serious face but he was looking directly in front of him, as if he was also thinking about what had happened that night. The way he had run to his freedom while everyone else was either being beaten, shot at or murdered. Kevin shook off that thought before he did or said something he would regret.

"You went and check Steve yet?" Kevin said.

Wendell shook his head. "You crazy? It have police

guarding him. I waiting for this whole thing to calm down first."

"Okay. What about Marcus?"

"Marcus? Kev! Marcus dead," Wendell said with a concerned look on his face, as if Kevin hadn't already got that news.

Kevin's face changed as reality surfaced. He sighed and looked away in an attempt to hide his emotions.

Out of the five of them, Kevin, Marcus and Sean had been the closest. They'd known each other as far back as primary school. They had even gone to the same high school and been through the worst together. They'd only met Steve on a job site about two years ago and then they'd met Wendell four months after when he had moved into the neighbourhood from Tobago. Nevertheless, they had all been inseparable.

"I know he dead. But I asking if you went and show respect to his family yet?"

"No." Wendell said and sat back down on the bed and sank his face into his palms.

"Kev, to be honest with you." He was speaking in a soft voice. "Since after the shooting, I eh leave the house. I kind of waiting for everything to calm down before doing anything."

"You can't be serious," Kevin said, in a soft but angry voice.

Wendell lifted his head and looked up at him.

"What you mean I can't be serious?" he said.

"Because one of our friends dead and the other one in hospital in a critical condition. So you can't be fucking serious about hiding away until everything calm down,"

Kevin answered.

Wendell looked at the scars on Kevin's face. He shook his head and laughed, bitterly.

"Yeah, you right. I guess everybody went through a lot, and, everything happened so fast. I couldn't believe all that would've take place. From the shootout to people getting killed and then you went missing. I just thought this thing was too serious. Is like, for the first time in my life I was so scared." Kevin understood what he was saying. For him it had become like a natural reflex. There were so many times he was scared for his life over the weekend. It wasn't a good feeling at all, but it was what had helped him survive. There were things he'd done that he would've never done if he hadn't become so afraid of dying and was willing to do anything and everything to survive.

Wendell looked as though his mind was becoming distant. He was in deep thoughts.

Kevin remembered the moment before it all started. The way Christine was acting and looking around while in the car park. He was beginning to feel like such a fool for not suspecting that she was up to something. His best friend was dead and she was the person responsible. And, worst of all, Kevin knew it was partly his fault.

Within that moment he was contemplating on how to move forward and get his life back to normal. He wanted to tell Wendell about the corrupt police officers in the forest, but decided that it wasn't the right time.

"So, what now?" Wendell asked. Kevin shook his head. "I have no idea. I need some time to think." He leaned against the chest of drawer that was across from where Wendell was sitting.

"I didn't hear anything concerning the shooting on the news tonight."

"Yeah, me neither. I does pay attention to the news on mornings and evenings, but I didn't hear anything since the day after the shooting."

"Okay, that should be good."

"Well, we can't be too sure."

"Yeah, true. What you tell yuh mother though?"

Wendell sat up and looked at Kevin. "That we was liming and we end up getting in a fight with a group of fellas."

"Okay, and that was all?"

"Yeah."

Kevin was a bit surprised. "So, you didn't tell she who the fellas was and how this whole thing started?"

"No, she didn't want to know all that. She was upset."

"Yeah, knowing yuh mother, I could imagine."

"She want me to go and spend some time with my father in Tobago though."

"Okay, and what you plan to do?"

"I don't have a choice."

Kevin wasn't surprised this time.

"When you leaving?"

"Month end."

"Okay."

Kevin was thinking about the whole situation and the way it was destroying the entire crew and their families. There wasn't any way to fix it. The only thing left to do was adjust to the change and move on, and that was exactly what he was going to do.

"What ward Steve on?"

"Surgical ward three. I not sure which room."

"Okay. Mount Hope?"

"Yeah."

Kevin looked at the time. It was almost midnight and transportation would be getting difficult, forcing him to walk a long distance to get home. He told Wendell he was going to leave and Wendell got up to walk him out.

"When you plan on going in the hospital?"

"I not sure yet, maybe sometime over the weekend."

"Okay. Just be careful."

"Yeah, I know."

They came out of the room. Karen was asleep on the couch.

"Once I get a phone tomorrow I would call and you would get the number, okay?"

"Yeah man, no problem. Later."

"Yeah, later. Be safe."

Kevin left and walked out of the neighbourhood the same way he came in.

There were still people liming on the street corners but not as many as before. He got to the main road where he hailed a taxi within a few minutes, which took him straight to his apartment.

CHAPTER SIX

The rest of the week was quiet. Kevin stayed home and did nothing except watch movies and sleep, waiting for the weekend to visit Steve in the hospital.

He spoke to Shantel every day—she said she was doing well.

Wendell hadn't called, and Kevin wondered if he was still too scared to leave his house.

There still wasn't anything on the news or in the newspapers concerning the incidents that had taken place, so Kevin started feeling safe enough to live a normal life again.

On Saturday afternoon he left home and arrived at the hospital just after four o'clock. Visiting hours were between four and six o'clock.

When he went to reception, the clerk told him that Steve was in room 301 of the surgical ward, but also that extra security measures were in place for that patient and Kevin would have to present a photo ID before being allowed up and only one visitor would be allowed to see him.

While signing the book Kevin had noticed that Steve's family had been visiting him on a regular basis. His mom and sister had come yesterday afternoon and his father earlier today.

Kevin made his way up the steps and followed the directions he'd gotten from the clerk. In the last corridor he saw a police officer sitting on a chair outside the door next to the nurse's station. There he was asked to present his identification again, and a transmission was sent by the officer to his superiors before he'd gotten the okay to send him in.

"Go ahead," the officer said, after carefully searching him. Kevin pushed the door and entered the room.

Steve was the only patient in the room though there were three unoccupied beds.

He was partially covered in a white blanket and he had a cast on his right leg and arm and a bandage was wrapped around his chest.

There was a saline bag hanging from a metal rack beside Steve's bed and machines hooked up to his body were beeping.

The room carried that unique hospital smell that reminded Kevin why he hated hospitals so much. His only hope was that he wouldn't be exposed to any blood or wounds while he was there.

There was a large window on the opposite side of the door, but Steve's full attention was on the TV, which had a crime watch programme on. He looked around when the door thumped shut, and his eyes grew bright when he saw Kevin.

"Aye," Steve said.

"Oh buddy, what going on?" Kevin said and walked to the bed. Steve attempted to smile.

"You alive?" he said

"I guess so." Kevin rested his hand on Steve's. "I get a lil beat up, but I good to go."

Steve looked at him from head to toe. "I realize."

"Yeah, well. You know how it is. I see you not doing so bad yourself."

"Yeah." Steve's voice got a little stronger. "Four bullets. I thought I was dead until I wake up in this place, covered with bandage and tubes." He shifted around his body to get in a more relaxed position on the bed.

"I see you hire police!" Kevin said, grinning.

"Yeah, you laugh. Is your tax dollars that paying them."

"Yeah, I hear you."

Kevin laughed, and Steve tried to do the same, but it seemed painful.

Kevin was paying attention to the crime programme on the TV for a while and when he looked back at Steve he saw that he was staring at him as if he had something on his mind.

"What?" Kevin said.

"Nothing really. I was just thinking about how things was in the past."

"Okay."

"You know. The way we meet at that construction site and how you kind of stick around like a little brother ever since." His voice was beginning to sound depressed. "The only thing I regretting is how I led you astray. Both you and Sean."

Kevin began thinking back also.

"If it wasn't for me, you woulda never have to go through all this. I mean, is not like we was murderers or gangsters or anything. But I should've never make allyuh come along on that scene with Biggs." He paused and looked at Kevin, trying to read his expression. Kevin turned away from his stare. "What I really trying to say is, sorry for everything."

Kevin looked back at Steve. He could feel his emotions rising. He understood what Steve was saying and he knew it was his decision to hang out with Steve and the crew. Whether Steve was selling on the block or making his pickup, or packaging his weed. For some strange reason Kevin accepted that type of company and the little money there was to gain from it. He was out of a job and sadly that was how he'd managed to spend his time.

"Hmm," Kevin sighed. "I really don't know what to say, but I guess everybody responsible for their own decisions at the end of the day. It sad that it have to turn out like this. But, I know that is how life is. We win some, we lose some." After dwelling on the past it was hard for Kevin to hold himself together so he took a walk over to the window where he stood looking out in silence. He returned a few minutes after.

"How everything shaping up with you otherwise?" Kevin asked, changing the mood. Steve looked satisfied that he'd gotten it off his chest. He delayed for a few seconds before answering.

"Well, this is my life right here. So far they still have me down as the victim since they don't have anything to work with, and I gave so much statements I starting to feel like a celebrity."

"Celebrity, eh?"

"Well, you know what ah mean," Steve chuckled.

"No, not really, but I listening."

"Yeah," he continued. "I have police, doctors and nurses on a twenty-four hour basis, so things safe and shaping up. I can't complain."

"Or, okay. But, you did mention anything about Biggs?" Kevin asked.

"Nah." Steve looked angry. "I will handle that for myself when I come out from here."

Kevin was shocked by his intentions. He thought about what Shantel had told him of not seeking revenge and he realized that the both of them lived two completely different lives. Steve had no one to live for but himself which would make it easy for him to think that way. Kevin even realized that things were only getting more serious, from the ambush to the shooting, and now Steve planning to kill someone. Kevin was glad that he had made the decision to go separate ways.

The room was becoming too quiet and Kevin thought about saying anything that would start a conversation again.

"Well, I see you getting regular visits. So, that good."

It took Steve a moment before he answered. "Yeah, my father does come every day with food and fruits."

Kevin recognized a box of food on a tray at the side of the bed. There was also a plastic bag with two bananas, an apple, and some grapes.

"What, things better than home?" Kevin teased.

"I wouldn't say so. You smell this place?"

Kevin was reminded of the methylated spirits mixed with urine scent he had been trying to ignore from the moment he walked in.

"Well, it doesn't smell nice. But look at the bright side. It could've be much worse. You could be unguarded and in the company of them three patients." Kevin pointed to the three empty beds.

"True."

They fell silent and Steve's eyes went back to the TV. Kevin cleared his throat.

"What about Wendell?" he said.

Steve turned his head. "What about him?"

"He come to visit?" Kevin asked, although he already knew the answer.

Steve shook his head.

"No. The last time I see him was some minutes before the shooting."

Kevin frowned. "Before?"

"Yeah, well, he went to use the washroom. That was right before the bouncer come and tell we what was going on outside. Me and Marcus came running out and I eh hear or see him since."

"Hmm," said Kevin, his frown deepening.

"What happen?" Steve asked.

"Nothing really. I went by Wendell earlier this week and I just find it strange that he was looking okay. Not one cut or scratch or anything. I asked him how come and he say he ran away because he didn't have any weapon."

"Yeah, possibly."

"I know. But you know Wendell does never back down from a fight."

"True."

Kevin hesitated.

"You didn't notice him operating strange or anything?" he asked.

Steve shrugged.

"Nah, not really. He didn't go to the washroom much. That was maybe his second time, so I didn't find it strange. What I find strange is how much days pass and he still eh call or come to visit me. That not normal."

"Well, he say he lost he phone that same night during the scuffle. So maybe that is why he eh call. And, concerning the visit he say he waiting for this whole thing to clear up first."

Steve tried to sit up straighter in bed, but then winced in pain.

"Bullshit!" he said.

Kevin glanced around at the door, where the policeman was sitting outside. "Not so loud," he said.

"That is bullshit," Steve said again, lowering his voice. "First thing first, it didn't have any scuffle. We wasn't even close to Biggs and his boys. As soon as we see them throwing you in the car we started shooting from the entrance of the car park, and it don't have anything to calm down. I tell the police this whole thing started because of a girl in the club and it escalated when me and Marcus was outside organizing to leave. So his whole story covered in shit. He is a coward and it finally out in the open. I could barely wait to tell him that to his fucking face!" Steve turned, directing his anger outside the window.

Kevin noticed that the officer was standing and looking into the room. Steve simply ignored him.

Kevin looked at the time. It was 5:37. There was a commercial on the television and there were a lot of people walking back and forth in the corridor, both inside, and on the outside walkway.

"You alright, buddy?" Kevin asked after a short while.

"Yeah, no worries, I good," Steve answered with his head still facing the window.

A couple more minutes passed, and he finally looked back at Kevin.

"You realize I going to be here for a while, right?" Steve said.

"Yeah, judging from yuh condition I think that is understood."

"Okay, well. Until everything clear up with Wendell, you is the only person I could trust. I know you done say you want out and I not asking you to do anything out of the way." He studied Kevin's expression to make sure they were both on the same page.

"Yeah, okay," Kevin nodded. "What you want me to do?"

"Okay, come closer," he said in a low voice while making similar gestures.

Kevin looked around and then leaned closer to him.

"The stuff in the same place?" he whispered.

"Yeah. Well, I hope so."

"Okay. I need you to move it. Call Charles and liaise with him. It don't matter where allyuh put it. Just move it. Is plenty stuff and if things don't turn out the way I expecting it to, I don't want Wendell getting his hands on it."

Kevin agreed, though he knew it would be a bit difficult to find another location. Steve told him where he would find the key.

"Thanks, bro." Steve stuck out his hand and received a fist bump.

"Yeah, no problem." Kevin nodded and straightened up. He knew he was going against his intentions, but he also knew that this was a difficult time for everyone and it was the least he could do.

At that same moment there was an interruption on the TV that caught their attention.

It was 5:45 and instead of having a news update, the reporter came on and announced that there was breaking news on the Arima nightclub shooting.

Kevin looked around as he heard the volume on the television at the nurse's station turned up and the officer moved in closer.

Kevin was becoming worried and anxious. He folded his hands and placed his attention on the TV. His eyes then went from observing the officer's movement, to what was being said on the news and then to the window all in one quick movement. *Would he need a fast exit?* He wondered. After the reporter had finished introducing himself and the network he began with the breaking news.

"Today police have come up with a motive of the Arima nightclub's shooting, and has put the country on high alert for a lone male suspect who was involved in a shootout with police in the Brasso Seco forest earlier today."

Kevin couldn't move. As much as he wanted to look around at the officer it was as though his body was frozen in the direction of the TV. His heart was racing, and he was taking deep breaths. He had no idea what to expect. He knew he was involved in a similar incident with the police almost a week ago. Having another shootout earlier today with an alleged nightclub suspect couldn't be a coincidence.

Kevin was released from his trance and his eyes finally went into the corridor. He noticed that the officer was more focused on the television and he knew it might be the best opportunity he would get for a worst-case scenario.

He started walking casually to the door, trying not to draw the officer's attention.

Steve looked confused when he observed his actions and Kevin signaled him to remain quiet.

"The man," the reporter continued, "who is known as Kevin Jones of Kenneth Street, Enterprise."

Kevin turned to the screen when he heard the reporter say his name. He felt as though time froze along with his movements. On the television screen he could see his passport photograph blown up for the entire country to see.

He turned back just in time to see the officer staring at him.

The officer reached for his firearm and Kevin slammed the door shut and locked it from the inside.

"Stop!" the officer shouted. "Open this door!"

Kevin ran to the window, which was sealed shut. He could hear the officer turning the door handle, then kicking at the door.

"Kev, what going on?" Steve said with a confused face.

"I will explain everything. They trying to set me up."

"Open up this fucking door!" the policeman shouted again. Kevin grabbed a metal table from a corner of the room and began hitting the window pane until it shattered. The broken glass was scattered on both sides of the floor.

Kevin wasted no time in climbing over on to the outside corridor.

The ground was too far down so jumping was no longer an option. Kevin ran down the corridor with people scattering fearfully out of his way. He shoved aside those persons who didn't move fast enough.

There was a staircase next to the elevator and a security guard was sitting at a nearby desk. The guard stood up when he realized there was a commotion, but Kevin was already skipping steps as he fled. A crowd of people were milling around the bottom of the staircase. They were all looking up and taking pictures of the broken window. Three security officers were on the opposite side running in Kevin's direction.

"Stop him!" he heard the police officer shout out to the crowd as the officer ran down the corridor with two security officers behind him.

Kevin sprinted across the lawn in front of the main hospital to the adjoining buildings. He looked back and saw one of the security officers still on his trail. The other two were far behind, however, and the police officer was nowhere to be seen. He dashed behind the nearest building, finding himself running through knee-high bushes. There was a drain alongside him, covered with concrete slabs that led to a wire fence that protected the perimeter of the hospital and was crowned with barbed wire. Kevin had to make a choice. He'd have to either jump the fence and risk getting some nasty puncture wounds or go into the drain which had an unknown depth and could even get deeper before he reached the end.

He continued running at a slower pace while looking for a slab that could be shifted with the least amount of effort. He came up to one a couple metres down. He moved the slab aside, jumped into the drain and shifted it back into place.

Inside the drain was dark and smelled like a mixture of faeces and urine. He could also feel a lot of garbage floating in the cold water and rubbing against his feet. Rays of sunlight came through the small crease between every slab and when his eyes adjusted to the light he saw garbage and roaches and rats moving around him. His shoes and the base of his pants were already soaked. As he made his way through, the place got darker and the water level rose from his ankles to his knees. He couldn't see the end of the drain, but he could hear the water falling into a deeper drain.

He continued lifting his feet through until he was at the end and at that point he climbed down into the deeper and wider drain. The water was at his chest now and he kept his hands hovering above the water as garbage floated towards him. He kept his mouth closed and made his way towards the light at the opening. The air was warm, and the stench was becoming unbearable. For the last few metres it became difficult for him to breathe and Kevin felt as if he was about to faint.

He regained his strength when he heard cars speeding above him and also police sirens which sounded as though they were within the hospital's compound.

The drain had led to a bridge and Kevin held onto the railing and climbed out, looking around cautiously. There wasn't anyone close by. The only persons who saw him climbing out were the ones who were speeding by in cars and maxis on the bus route. Some people were waiting for the bus at a shed higher up, but they were paying attention to the commotion that was taking place inside the hospital and didn't notice the man who was climbing out of the drain.

Kevin's clothes were soaked, and he was stained with the scent of the sewage water. Sweat was also running down his face from all the running. He knew getting transportation out of the area in his condition would be an impossible task, so he kept moving.

The sun had disappeared, and the place was becoming dark. Kevin hoped that the night would bring some ease to his situation. He made his way into a quiet neighbourhood and ignored all passing vehicles as he took a brisk walk looking for a safe place to hide. He passed a lot of residential houses before noticing a half-built house to the top of the street. It was already covered with a roof, but there weren't any windows or doors. The grass around the house was very high and moss grew along the walls.

He looked around, making sure there weren't any passing vehicles and then crawled through the wire fencing and made his way into the house. As he walked through the rooms he could smell stale urine and he noticed graffiti on the walls. Plastic bags and old newspapers were also on the floor in one of the rooms. There was no telling how long the house had been abandoned, but it was evident that some homeless person was already using it as a shelter.

Kevin went to a room in the back that was far away from the scent and sat on the ground. He was prepared to stay awake and observant.

CHAPTER SEVEN

For nearly an hour blue flashing lights strobed on the walls around Kevin as the officers roamed the area in an intense search.

He heard a helicopter circling the area, but there wasn't any excessive barking coming from the neighbourhood dogs to suggest that the officers were making a house to house search.

Eventually, everything fell quiet. Kevin checked his watch—it was 8:35 p.m.

Suddenly, music started blasting from the house next to where he was hiding, and he stood up and walked into another room and looked through the window. The urine scent was stronger in this room, but he knew it was something he'd have to bear. He used his hand to block his face and tried to control his breathing. He stood at the window peeping out from an angle where he was perfectly hidden.

The house next door was a cream two-storey building and the music was coming from a car parked at the gate. They'd left the doors of the car open to get the best sound. There were four young men standing in the yard with beers in their hands. They were dressed and dancing, apparently ready to go clubbing. There was also a group of women in the porch, shouting at one another as if they were having a political debate at a bar. The only difference was that their faces were covered with smiles and whereas everyone was laughing.

Kevin remained at the window observing them. He kept looking at his watch, hoping that the neighbours would leave soon.

Then another car arrived at 9:55 p.m. and the guys carried a large cooler to one of the cars, together with a few cases of beers and four bottles of alcohol. Two of the men were walking in and out of the house, and Kevin figured that they were the ones who lived there. They also resembled each other, so he assumed they were related. A short while after, all the lights inside the house were switched off and the two young men came walking out with one of them locking the door. The girls got up and went to the cars, and eventually, all three cars drove off leaving a quiet neighbourhood behind once again.

Kevin waited a few more minutes to make sure nobody had forgotten anything, then went to the back of the house and climbed over the concrete fence and dropped into the yard. A large area around the house was cast in concrete and there was a wide strip of lawn alongside the fence. Around the house was dark, so Kevin walked to the back and sides looking for an easy entry point. But all the windows were secured with burglar-proofing. His only option was the front door; he had noticed that the lock on the burglar proof could be broken.

He went back into the abandoned house and brought back two flat pieces of steel to break open the door. It was more difficult than he thought but, after several frustrating attempts, the lock finally snapped, and the door swung open. He went in quickly and closed the door behind him.

Kevin wasted no time, making his way up the stairs. The upper floor had three bedrooms and a bathroom. He looked through the closet of one of the bedrooms and found a white T-shirt, and a jeans and a pair of sneakers in another room. He also took a backpack and packed two additional set of clothes. He then had a quick shower, got dressed and took the time to make a ham sandwich to eat on the way.

He dumped his dirty clothes in a bin before getting to the bus route. When he got out of the maxi in Curepe 30 minutes later, he was surprised by how lively the place looked. There were a lot of cars and taxis and people walking around. No one seemed to notice him. He walked to where the taxis were parked and approached a dark-skinned man who was leaning against an empty car. Kevin told him where he wanted to go, and the man agreed to take him there for a price that was rather high. But Kevin wasn't about to make money an issue.

It was a quiet drive except for the R&B music playing on the radio. At one point the driver asked about the scars on Kevin's face, but Kevin ignored him and continued looking out the window. There weren't any more questions after that.

They were making their way through a dirt track in Cunupia when Kevin felt the driver's eyes on him. He looked into the rear-view mirror and the driver looked away after their eyes met. The track had few streetlights and was lined with bushes. There were only two houses.

"How far again?" the driver asked.

"Not too far," Kevin answered. "You almost reach. We should be there in less than five minutes."

The car got quiet again.

"Right by this house you coming up to," Kevin said. He could sense the relief from the driver as he sped up and stopped in front of the house.

"Thanks again," Kevin said as he paid and got out of the car. The driver quickly turned the vehicle and drove out.

Kevin opened the gate and went into the yard. The house was a flat unpainted building that had belonged to Steve's uncle who had died two years before. It had no running water or electricity.

Kevin walked around the house and entered through the only door, which was to the back. There were only three rooms: a kitchen, a living room and a bedroom. A sofa in the living room and a mattress on the ground of the bedroom were the only items of furniture. Kevin turned on the three gas lamps that he and the guys had brought when they had first come to the house and placed one in each room.

He removed the sheet covering the sofa and decided that he would sit down for a while before going to check on the stuff since he was feeling very weak and tired from all the running around he had done. But he wanted to make sure that the items were still there, so he could ease his suspicion of Wendell having anything to do with the shooting.

He thought about the news report that had claimed the shooting had happened earlier that day, when it had in fact occurred almost a week ago. There was no doubt that the police were up to something. Kevin knew it would only be a matter of time before he was caught or, maybe, dead. His mind went to Shantel and what the police might do if they found out she was his girlfriend and where she was staying.

Those thoughts kept his mind occupied and he was beginning to feel uneasy. It was making it difficult for him to concentrate on anything else. He leaned back on the couch and stared at the wall with tears running down his cheeks. He was studying the whole situation and the way his life had changed in just a matter of days. He felt like a prisoner, invisible to the free world.

Within a short while his eyelids became heavy and he found himself fighting to stay awake. It was a battle he did not win.

CHAPTER EIGHT

Kevin's eyes opened to the sunlight that was coming through the fancy bricks that blocked the windows. He looked around, confused, taking a few seconds for his mind to adjust to the reality of where he was. He then sat upright and looked at his watch. It was already 8:15 a.m.

He got up and went into the kitchen. He climbed on the counter and retrieved the key from the spot beneath the galvanize roof as Steve had indicated. There was a pitchfork next to the door. He took it up and made his way outside, and although no houses were nearby, he looked around, making sure the coast was clear before walking a distance into the trees behind the house.

He stopped at the mango tree where they would gather all the grass after cleaning and started pushing the grass aside. There was an old rug underneath. He threw it aside and started digging. It was something they would've normally done together and he could remember the last time they were there as if it was yesterday. The way they had all cooperated with one another until placing the final shovel of dirt that buried their haul.

Within twenty minutes Kevin had reached the four feet depth and cleared the area around the steel trunk. He stuck the fork in the dirt and kneeled down next to the hole. Sweat was dripping from his forehead and arms and his clothes were now wet and dirty. He unlocked the steel trunk and lifted the lid.

Inside the trunk he could see the two revolvers, the shotgun, and the three packets of cocaine they had taken from Biggs and his gang. There were also some stacks of cash and some rounds. He didn't check it, but he was certain that it was the amount they had left. Although Steve was the only one who had access to the key, the five of them knew where the items were hidden, and it was their suspicion that had them worried, but nothing was missing.

He blew out a breath of relief and began laughing at the fact that he had actually thought Wendell had gone against them. But then he began feeling confused and frustrated again and he sat on the dirt with his hands resting on his forehead. Now that nothing was missing, it was hard to believe that Wendell had anything to do with the ambush, even though he hadn't been acting like himself lately. Maybe Steve was wrong. Maybe they were both wrong. Whatever it was, Kevin knew he had to decide whether he was going to trust him in the future or not.

He got up hoping to pull himself together while on his feet. There was no doubt that everything was happening too fast. But, the reality remained, and Kevin knew that he wouldn't be able to get through it alone. He was so accustomed to doing everything with the crew. They were his family and now his family was separated, and as Steve said, no one should be trusted. But that was easier said than done.

Kevin went into the house, retrieved the backpack and returned. He took one of the pistols and loaded a magazine with fifteen rounds and stuck both items into the bag. He then took up three stacks of the hundred-dollar bills which were wrapped in rubber bands and threw it in the backpack also. He closed the lid and secured the area just like he'd met it. He tidied up and was then ready to leave.

First, he would go to Charles's place as Steve suggested and organize for the items to be moved and then he would go to Wendell's house and hopefully they would come together and figure out a way for him to get out of his mess.

There was a shortcut to get to the main road. It was behind the house and across a river. It was a twenty minutes walk which they wouldn't do at night because of the pitch-black darkness. He made his way through the bushes and over the river, and by the time he had gotten to the main road his face and upper body was covered with sweat again.

From the first glance he noticed vehicles were speeding by and a lot of people were waiting for transportation. The sun was very hot. He waited on the opposite side of the road, hoping to draw less attention, or none at all. After a few minutes a maxi pulled up and some of the persons standing across the street fought their way in. This happened several times until there were only four persons left. They were all lucky enough to get into the next maxi that pulled up, and Kevin boarded as well.

A half-hour later, he was at the top of the street where Charles lived. It was a quiet neighbourhood, so he didn't have to worry much about being noticed. From a few houses away he could see Charles outside, putting his police uniform and other items into his car.

Charles was attached to a task force unit at a station in the East. Steve and Charles were neighbours and childhood friends and they had been inseparable in the past. This was until they were introduced to the community drug leader and unlike Steve, Charles had decided to join the Protective Services instead of working on the streets. They hadn't seen each other for a while but they had kept in regular communication via phone calls. Charles's loyalty had been proven and his trust had never been an issue for Steve, and that made all the difference.

Charles noticed Kevin and quickly stuck everything into the car, and when Kevin got closer to him, he shook his head slightly and gestured for Kevin to follow him inside. When they got inside Charles closed the door behind them and peeped out his window to make sure none of his neighbours were outside to notice when Kevin came in. The place was dark and he turned on the light.

"What going on with you?" Charles said with a curious and concerned expression. Kevin kept his face blank. His eyes were locked on Charles who was looking right back at him.

"What going on?" Charles asked again in a more demanding voice. "All of a sudden I hearing about this shooting at the party and now I seeing yuh face all over the news. I even call Steve yesterday and he and all shock.

He say you was there with him and when the news come on you caused one big commotion and run out of the hospital."

Kevin shook his head and started walking towards the couch which was only a few feet away.

"Hmm… I really don't know what to tell you." He took a seat and Charles sat on the opposite couch.

"What you mean you don't know what to tell me?" he gestured, expressing his confusion. "Tell me what going on. Tell me why you starring on the news. At least tell me something."

"Is not that. I know what going on, I just don't know if, or how to explain it."

"If?" Charles elaborated on the word and shook his head. "What? You don't trust me or something?"

"No, yeah. Well, you know what I mean."

"No, I don't know what you mean." Charles was becoming angry and Kevin knew that he'd have to calm him down before things got out of control.

"Listen. For them past few days I went through all kind of torture. I just real tired and frustrated, and it real hard to figure out who to trust."

He noticed Charles shook his head again with a confused look on his face. "What you mean you don't know who to trust? What you doing here then, if you having second thoughts."

"Steve tell me to come here. Apparently you is the only officer he would trust."

"I know, and I don't blame him. We go way back and he was always like a brother to me, and I never going to forget that."

Kevin looked across to where Charles was sitting. His face was as serious as a judge passing a death penalty.

"Look, I just need a minute to think, alright."

"Yeah, and I was late for work, but yet I come back inside. You know why? Because family comes first, and everything else comes after."

Kevin absorbed everything Charles was saying, and he realized why Steve had kept him close. He spoke like a true brother. It made Kevin wonder what their childhood was like.

Kevin rubbed his hands through his hair. "Yeah, you right. I don't even know where to start though."

"Start by telling me, exactly what went on?" Charles said.

Kevin lowered his head and started thinking. He was very much aware of the position he was in, and he was beginning to realize that for the next few days he'd have to be making quick decisions on who he should or could not trust, and why. He also knew that he'd have to be reliving his experiences as if explaining a movie to someone who had never heard of it before. Nevertheless, if it was worth getting out of his situation, he was willing to do both.

He looked across to Charles and started explaining how he was being framed. He told him about the drug house and what he'd seen on the footage. He didn't mention anything about leaving with the memory card. It was the most concrete evidence he had to fight his case and he wasn't about to mention it to anyone without the assurance that they were down with him, one hundred percent.

"And what this have to do with the shooting at the club?"

"Nothing." Kevin brushed away the thought. "Is two different things. You remember the altercation that Steve did call you about some weeks ago?"

Charles was thinking. "You mean when he did take the drugs from that fella?"

"Yeah."

"Okay, yeah, I remember. What happen?"

"That is Biggs. It was his drugs. He come by the club with the intentions of getting it back, or getting some kind of revenge. They beat me up and throw me in their car and I manage to get away, and that is how I run into the drug house."

"Oh, okay. So, you saying that all this didn't take place yesterday?"

"No. Everything happen the same night with the shooting at the club, and the day after."

"Hmm..." Charles looked as if he was having a hard time getting up to speed. "So why the news say it happened yesterday?"

"I don't know. Maybe, because after having their little reunion, they find it would be the best way to get to me."

Kevin was becoming annoyed by how slow the explanation process was progressing. He was running out of time and from the way things was sounding, he was getting the impression that Charles wouldn't be able to help in any way. He stood up and started pacing back and forth in an attempt to clear his head. Charles slouched back on the sofa.

"You know you could calm down right?" he said to Kevin. "I just asking these questions to try and understand what really going on."

"Calm down for what?" Kevin said in a loud aggressive voice. He was too frustrated and scared to remain calm and it was as if Charles wasn't understanding that. He noticed Charles biting down on his jaw, trying to hold back his anger. Charles got up and went to the kitchen and opened the refrigerator, taking out a bottle of water and drinking straight from it. Kevin was too angry to apologize for the way he was carrying on, and the tension made the room quiet for a while.

"Listen." Kevin went back to his seat. "I really need some kind of advice here. I don't know how long again I could manage to be running around like this. Ah don't even know who I could trust. But I trust Steve and he trust you, even though you is one of them. That is the only reason why I sitting here now. Ah don't even know what going on with Wendell. I try calling him and his phone ringing out and going straight to voice mail."

"Yeah, I tried calling him yesterday too, before I called Steve, and the same thing happen," Charles said. "You sure everything okay with him?"

Kevin smiled and shook his head. "Yeah, he good. Not a single scratch."

Charles' eyes opened wide.

"What?" He was surprised. "You serious? Through all that?"

"Yeah, I went by his house sometime late last week, and he looking the same way he was looking before the shooting."

"Hmm." Charles slowly shook his head. "That strange."

"Yeah. That was Steve reaction too."

Kevin took a moment to remind himself that nothing was missing from their hideout and comforted his mind by thinking that maybe Wendell hadn't yet purchased a new phone like he said, which was a bit hard to believe since social media was Wendell's main hobby.

"So, based on everything I tell you, what you think I should do, from a police point of view?"

Charles came back from the kitchen and sat down on the couch.

"Well, when you think about it, they have you down as a fugitive on the news, so everybody would be seeing you as a fugitive whether you like it or not. So right now the best thing for you to do is surrender."

"You really think that is the only choice I have?"

"Well, yeah. Things could end up a lot worse if you continue hiding."

Kevin knew he was telling the truth. He remembered the conversation the corporal was having with the other officers at the drug house before he escaped, and it was obvious that they'd rather have him dead than alive.

"I don't like that idea too much."

"What, to surrender?"

"Yeah."

Charles laughed and looked up to the ceiling as if he was searching for the right words. "Remember you asked for advice from a police point of view? That is why I tell you that would be the easiest way out. Cause I know how police does think."

"Yeah, but I want to be one hundred percent sure that something would come out of this, and it wouldn't really reach far if I behind bars."

"So, you feel you would do a better job if you out there running wild?"

"Not running wild, but if I could orchestrate a plan somehow."

"Hmm." It had him thinking. "So what you have in mind?"

Kevin thought about it before answering. "What about if I make a deal to take the police to the drug house and explain to the judge that, that was the reason behind everything?"

"Hmm, that could work, but you would have to know who is who. Remember, police does stand up for each other."

"Yeah, true. But what about police complaints?"

"Same thing. Once a police looking bad it does put a image on the entire Service. Everybody would want to cover up something that big."

"Even you?"

Kevin saw Charles's face change. "I not even sure," Charles said. "I would try to help you as much as possible, but I can't promise you anything. Plus, I wouldn't be able to manage something like this by myself. And we not even sure the kind of persons involved."

"Yeah, that is true. It have plenty soldiers in this thing too."

"See what I saying?"

Kevin nodded.

They both continued thinking in silence. Charles was looking at the time on his watch every now and then and Kevin remembered that he had mention he was already late for work.

"You know what!" Charles broke the silence and jumped up, taking his phone out of his pocket before falling back onto the couch. "While we just sitting here let me call somebody from the station who might have ah better input in this whole thing." He was looking more confident than he had been during their entire conversation.

He started dialing the number but Kevin stopped him. "Who you calling?" he asked.

Charles explained that he was calling the superintendent for their division who would have more information. He was also the person who arranged all the police exercises for the district. When the question was asked about trust, Charles said that the superintendent was a no-nonsense person and he would trust him with his life.

Although Kevin was a bit skeptical about getting so much police involved, Charles's elaboration on the officer's loyalty was enough for Kevin to go along with it.

Charles contacted the superintendent and placed the call on speaker so Kevin would hear what was being said. They had a lengthy conversation, as Charles filled him in on the details.

"So, he there with you now?" the superintendent said.

"No, he not here right now." Charles said. "Actually, he was never here. He call me earlier today and tell me everything."

The superintendent asked a few more questions and Kevin was satisfied with the way the conversation was going until the superintendent suggested that it would be wise for Kevin to surrender before the situation got out of hand.

"But sir, remember I tell you, I know this fella since I small. He don't have no record or any problem with the police. He not capable of doing something like that."

"Yes, Charles. I hearing everything you saying, but you have to keep in mind that, people does change."

"Yeah, I know that. But not him. I know what I telling you. What about the drug house?"

"What about it?"

"He wouldn't just make up something like that. Let we still go and see what going on with that and deal with it."

The superintendent was quiet for a while. If it wasn't for the tapping sound that finally came from his end of the phone, they would've believed that the call had been dropped.

Charles told him about the possible quantity of drugs and money that could be confiscated and the publicity, and he liked the idea.

"Okay, here what I would do," said the superintendent. "I would arrange for Sergeant Joseph and his men to take allyuh to the location and back." They heard him take a deep breath before continuing. "Charles?"

"Yes sir."

"I taking a big chance here. You stay close to him and make sure he in handcuffs the entire time. And take him straight to the Arima station afterwards, okay?"

"Yes sir. Thank you so much. Would do." Charles was looking at Kevin while speaking. The superintendent hung up right after.

Kevin thought about it and although it wasn't what

he had expected. It was basically both of their ideas joining as one, so he had no problem with the arrangements. The one thing he wanted out of the situation was to know that the officer's corruption would come to an end and he knew he would have a better opportunity to clear his name once that happens.

He thanked Charles for everything and Charles told him that he could stay at his place for the night and then he left for work.

CHAPTER NINE

The last thing Charles said to him before leaving, was to make himself at home and he did just that. The house had two furnished bedrooms in addition to the kitchen, living room, bathroom and dining room. Kevin moved through each room, examining the furnishings and comparing Charles's lifestyle to Steve's. There was no doubt that Charles had come out better.

After his tour through the house he went back to the living room. Magazines were scattered on the coffee table, and he noticed a Guns and Ammo magazine on top. He took it up and began flipping the pages. Kevin didn't know much about guns and he could easily count the number of times he had carried a firearm on the fingers on one hand. He wasn't very good at shooting either. He had gone to an open field with the crew on two occasions and he couldn't hit anything that was further than ten feet. He shook his head at the thought, knowing very well that he was carrying a weapon he couldn't use. He put the magazine back on to the coffee table and got up and picked up Charles's landline phone. He hadn't spoken to Sean a few days now, and he knew he'd be worried after seeing him on the news last night. He also wanted to update him on what was going to take place tomorrow.

He dialed the number and when Keisha answered she was very anxious to transfer the call this time. Kevin leaned against the kitchen counter, waiting.

"Kevin, what going on with you, boy?" Sean said in a sort of panic. His tone took Kevin by surprise.

"Well, I still alive. What going on?"

"Yeah, you alive, thank God. But what going on with this shooting thing? It all over the news. And since when you shooting behind people?"

"Sean, you of all people know me better than that."

"Well, that is what I saying, but when I see this on the news, I was shock. In fact, everybody up here shock."

Kevin could only imagine what Sean's cousins were saying and thinking about him. It also made him wonder how he would be seen in the public's eyes.

"But, you don't believe it, right?" Kevin said.

Sean answer came immediately. "Of course not. I know you better than that. And, I remember what you was telling me the other night. So, I know they would say and do whatever they could to catch up with you."

Kevin felt good to know that Sean was still on his side.

"Where you is now?"

"I by Charles."

"Charles?" He could sense the concern in Sean's voice.

"Yeah, what happen?"

"Nah, nothing." There was a short pause. "How you

manage to go there with everything that taking place with you and them police?"

"Well, to be honest. It was Steve's idea."

"Hmm, no wonder. Allyuh brave yes." He ended in a low voice, almost as if he was speaking to himself.

"It don't have nothing to do with being brave. Right about now I just trying to stay alive."

Kevin noticed that the hand he was holding the phone with was becoming cold and sweaty. He transferred the phone to the other hand and wiped his palm on his pants.

"What Charles had to say about all this?"

"Well, I tell him everything and he call some senior officer who arrange for we to go back to the drug house tomorrow."

"Alright, and you okay with that, right?"

"Well, kinda. I mean. I ah little worried about how things would play off. But I done here already and I feeling like is the only choice I have."

Sean remained quiet for a moment.

"You think that drug house would still be there though? I mean with all this drama going on, I doubt they would take that kind of risk."

Sean had made a valid point. This was actually the first time that Kevin had thought about them destroying the drug house in order to protect themselves. It would be the easiest way out. And, if it was so, it would definitely weaken Kevin's case.

Kevin thought about it long and hard and then made up his mind that he would go through with it, regardless. He knew it was a greater risk going back out there, where they were all searching for him.

"Kevin, you still there?"

"Yeah, I right here." He tightened his grip on the phone.

"You hear what I now say?"

"Yeah, I hear you."

"And you okay with that?"

"Well, at the end of the day, it is a risk I would have to take."

"Hmm, okay… true. Well, that is up to you."

They were both quiet for a few seconds and then Kevin asked if he knew when he was coming back home.

"Well, with all this bacchanal going on, I done organize to come back over the weekend," Sean said.

"Okay good. Because I need to be around somebody I could trust, and you would be more help than Wendell."

"Why you say that? What happen? You eh get through to him yet?"

"No. I didn't call since the news come across yesterday evening. But before that, I wasn't getting through at all."

Kevin had thought about mentioning his visit to Wendell's house but decided not to. It was the only way Sean would realize that his back was against a wall and he was in desperate need of his assistance.

"Oh, okay. Well I don't know what to say, but when I come home I would see what going on with that."

"Okay, cool."

The phone was quiet again and when Kevin was about to say good bye, Sean asked about the drugs and other stuff at the hideout.

"Yeah, everything still there. Just like how we leave it."

"Alright, so Wendell didn't move anything then."

Kevin wasn't sure if he was asking a question or making an assumption. But, he told him no.

"Okay, well. That is good news. But don't worry. As soon as I come back I would find out if Wendell had anything to do with this. And, if that is the case. I sorry to say, but allyuh would be vex with me." Kevin could hear the pain and anger in Sean's voice. He knew exactly what he meant by that.

Kevin acknowledged the fact that they were all good friends, but if Wendell had anything to do with the shooting at the club, he'd deserve whatever came to him. At this stage, Kevin could care less.

"You good for the night?" Sean asked after some time passed.

"Yeah, I good." He looked around and reminded himself of the luxury of the house. "Don't worry about me."

"Alright, well, make sure and handle yuh business skillful. I would be moving with this phone, so if anything come up just give me a buzz, okay?" Sean said and hung up after Kevin's reply.

Kevin lay down on the couch, thinking, and quickly fell asleep.

CHAPTER TEN

Kevin sat in the front passenger seat of the car that Charles had rented. He was anxious and afraid about how the day was going to turn out.

The car was parked in a dirt track, close to the bus shed where Kevin had gotten the first bus out of Brasso Seco a week ago.

Charles sat to his right dressed in tactical pants and boots. His jacket and bullet proof vest were in the back seat. They were running late since the arrangement was to meet twenty minutes ago, however, Charles had called someone who confirmed that they were close by.

After a few more minutes, three marked police vehicles pulled up in front of them. Charles threw on his jacket and bullet proof vest and waited until the doors opened and when the nine officers came out he approached them.

They were all dressed in tactical wear like Charles, with bulletproof vest and knee pads and elbow pads. They looked as if they were prepared to fight a war with their guns across their chest and legs.

They'd formed a semi-circle around Charles and began conferring. After a few minutes, Charles signaled for Kevin to join them.

"Morning," one of the officers said and gave him a stern stare. "I is Sergeant Joseph. Don't worry about introducing yourself, I does watch news, so I done know who you is."

Kevin was taken aback by his insulting approach.

"Before we go further, I want you to understand something. Nobody here is yuh friend. This is business and strictly business. We train to follow instructions and that is all we doing. You understand that, right?"

"Yeah," Kevin nodded.

"Okay, good. So, you have some information for we?"

Charles was quietly standing at the outside of the circle.

"Yeah," Kevin said.

"Alright. And to add to what I now tell you. This is what we train to do, so don't get worried. If it have to turn ugly, it will get ugly. We enjoy this shit." His face was serious.

Kevin remained quiet this time.

Sergeant Joseph asked a few questions about the location of the drug house and the number of persons who had been there, and Kevin answered to the best of his knowledge, using his personal encounter and what he saw on the video footage to guide him.

"Okay, that should be it." He looked around at each officer, getting a few nods. He then looked at Charles.

"You search him?"

Kevin froze on hearing the question. His neck and shoulders felt tensed. Kevin was carrying the pistol on his waist without Charles's knowledge. Before leaving Charles's house, he had contemplated whether or not he should carry the firearm and had finally decided to. He kept his eyes away from Charles knowing very well that his answer could determine how this whole operation would go down.

Charles looked at Kevin and then turned to Joseph and answered with a yes.

The sergeant studied Charles face for a moment. The hesitation had obviously brought doubt to his mind.

One of the officers took a step forward to conduct the search, but the sergeant raised his hand, stopping him in his tracks.

"Alright, good." The sergeant finally said and turned away. He had spared him the embarrassment.

Kevin finally exhaled.

"Now that we pass that stage, how about if we go straight to planning a strategy?"

"Okay," Kevin said.

Joseph started instructing his men. The plan was that Kevin would stay in the leading vehicle with him and Charles in the vehicle to the end of the convoy. Kevin didn't like being separated from Charles, but he said nothing. The police team drove out of the track, leaving the rental behind. Kevin started giving directions.

They followed the road and made a few turns and when Kevin came to the village he began feeling as if he had been pressured by the officers.

"We almost reach?" Sergeant Joseph was looking at

him from the rear-view mirror.

"We have a little distance again to go." Kevin answered.

Joseph waited a short while and then he stuck his hand out of the window and signaled to the vehicles behind. The two officers on Kevin sides began checking their rifles.

The sergeant and the officer in the driver's seat did the same with their pistols.

They reached the spot where he had pushed the police vehicle down the precipice and he told Joseph that they were almost there and pointed to the end of the road where the drug house could be seen beyond the trees.

"Okay, good," Joseph said, and they proceeded slowly while scanning the area carefully.

When they were a few seconds away, two officers came out of each vehicle and began walking alongside them.

Kevin could feel his heart racing as he anticipated the moment. He counted down the seconds in his mind.

They came off the road and after passing the tall trees that created a fence, Kevin saw the drug house. It looked exactly the same.

He saw the broken window upstairs and he could see the broken chair and pieces of glass on the ground below it. All the vehicles came to a stop and his eyes were glued on an excavator on his left, in the spot where the truck and the police vehicles had been parked. The excavator was military green and it look as if they were planning on demolishing the building sometime soon. Kevin realized if he had come at a later day there was a possibility that the house would've been destroyed just as Sean had predicted.

Sergeant Joseph and everyone else exited the vehicles and Kevin followed.

"So this is the place?" Joseph asked.

"Yeah," Kevin answered.

Although the place looked deserted a few officers started moving around the perimeter of the building.

"Clear!" one of the officers shouted from the left side of the building and the three officers on the other sides said the same, as if they were his echo.

They remained where they were, and three other officers started moving towards the front window.

One of the officers was holding a metal case in his hand that was the size of a lunch kit. He remained in a crouching position on one side of the window and another officer was on the opposite side. He opened the kit and when the officer broke the glass he threw three cans at different angles inside the building. Kevin saw the building become clouded with smoke, then the officers pulled down their gas masks and entered through the window. They vanished in the smoke.

Kevin heard a similar noise and saw more smoke escaping through the windows upstairs.

About five minutes after he saw one of the officers appear at the top window and indicated that the building was empty. The front door opened shortly after and the sergeant moved towards the building after the smoke had cleared. Kevin, Charles and the other officer followed.

They entered the storage room and the sergeant stopped and observed the metal tables.

The officer who had gone in with them began taking a few pictures and Sergeant Joseph walked to the other room where the similar metal tables were located.

"It had drugs in this room too?" he asked.

"Yeah," Kevin answered.

They made their way throughout the entire building and Kevin explained what took place in each room from what he had seen. When they were finished, they all left the building and Sergeant Joseph contacted the superintendent and described everything that he had observed. He told him that nothing illegal was found and that no one was there.

"Okay," the sergeant said when he finished his call. Everyone was around him except the officers who were guarding the perimeter.

"I call Rampersad and tell him what went on. So, we have to take the suspect into custody like what we originally planned, and when we get back to base I would take back accordingly, okay."

"So what going to happen there?" Kevin asked.

"Well, we would use the information we get here and the investigators would question you, but I not sure which way it would go from there. You have to keep in mind that, at the end of the day, we didn't find any solid evidence, but the soldiers would have to answer for this." He pointed to the excavator.

"As long as they could give a good enough reason for it being here, you might very well be on your own. It don't have no footage or anything, so it would be a difficult case for you to fight."

He started walking back to the police vehicle and all

of the officers followed. The officers who were guarding the perimeter walked the vehicles back out to the beginning of the road before entering.

Kevin sat in the back seat between both officers and remained quiet. He was glad that they'd made the journey to the drug house, but he was disappointed that there wasn't anyone or anything there. He knew that during his court hearing he'd have to find a way for the judge to view the video. That was his only option now.

The vehicles were all speeding through the forested area when Sergeant Joseph signaled to the driver to slow down. Kevin began looking across his shoulders and wondering what was wrong.

Both officers stuck their rifles out of the window, prepared to shoot.

The sergeant waited a while and then give the driver the signal to proceed and stuck his hand out of the window, showing a similar signal to the vehicles behind. At that very instant, Kevin heard several loud noise like gunshots and the vehicle started swerving as the driver struggled to take control.

Kevin heard more gunshots being fired at the vehicles behind and before he could turn around, their vehicle ended up in the bushes just to the side of the road and the second vehicle came crashing into them, pushing them off the road and into a tree.

The officers dived out of the vehicles and went flat on the ground and started firing back.

Kevin struggled to stay low while attempting to exit the vehicle. The shooting stopped and he fell out the vehicle, hands first, and kept his body as low as possible and used his hands to shield his head.

When the shooting had stopped completely, and he finally opened his eyes he saw the sergeant lying on his stomach and scanning the area in front of him with his rifle.

Kevin had no idea where the shooting was coming from and he was too afraid to lift his head or turn around. A few moments passed and when he saw Sergeant Joseph get on one knee, he turned around and saw that all the other officers were taking cover behind the vehicles in a similar posture.

Joseph looked around and then shouted out to the vehicle in the back and one of the officers shouted back that Greg was hit. Kevin realized that it had started all over again and that the persons running the drug house were making it clear that nothing and no one was going to take them down. Sergeant Joseph crawled across to the other vehicle, keeping his head down. Kevin went flat on his chest and kept his eyes towards the vehicle where Joseph was heading. One officer was lying on his back on the safe side of the vehicle, and Charles and two others were surrounding him with a first-aid kit. Their hands and clothes were bloody.

The two other officers were covering the open sides of the vehicle. When the sergeant reached them he took over. The three of them remained with the wounded officer for almost fifteen minutes before Joseph made it clear that he'd have to be rushed to the hospital. They left him there and covered the drivers while they checked the vehicles.

Only two of the vehicles were accessible so the remaining officers would have to sit in the back.

Charles signaled for Kevin to come towards them, but Kevin ignored him, pretending to be afraid. The Sergeant said something to Charles and as he ran across to Kevin, three shots were fired from somewhere in the bushes. The officers all started firing into the area from where the shots came.

"Come, we have to go!" Charles said and held on to Kevin's arm.

"No," Kevin said and pulled away.

"What?" Charles' eyes opened wide and Kevin saw more fear than curiosity.

"I not going."

"What? What you mean you not going? Come!" Charles pulled him by his arm again and he pulled away with a lot more force.

"No. I not going."

"Why you acting like this?"

"I have the footage."

Charles looked confused now.

"What you talking about? What footage?"

"The one from the drug house. I have it. That is what they want."

Charles face was angry, and he kept sharing his focus between Kevin and the other officers. More shots fired towards them and both Kevin and Charles lay flat while the officers returned fire.

"Why the hell you didn't tell me that before, instead of getting all these people involve in this shit?"

Kevin looked at him and shook his head like a confused child. It was hard for him to concentrate with everything that was taking place around them.

"Charles? Why you taking so fucking long? We have to go now," Sergeant Joseph shouted.

"I don't know," Kevin finally answered. "I thought this way woulda work out better."

"Well you waste that fucking thought. Next time leave the thinking to the professionals."

Charles looked towards the sergeant again and then looked back at Kevin.

The wounded officer was already in the vehicle and they were waiting for Charles in order for everyone to get in and drive away at the same time.

"Come, I would get the footage," Charles said.

"No." Kevin shook his head. "If they willing to kill a police, who is me?" He pulled the gun from his waist in one quick motion and pointing it at Charles. Charles' eyes opened wide. As much as Kevin didn't want to do it, his life had become all about taking risks.

"You done do enough. I would get it, and..."

"Charles, we leaving in the next five seconds, with or without you," the sergeant shouted.

"Give me the keys."

"We don't have to go through this," Charles started saying.

"I don't care about all that, just give me the keys."

Charles shook his head and dipped his hand into his pocket, taking out the keys for the car.

"After everything I do for you, this is how you going to repay me?"

Kevin didn't want to think about all that. He ignored everything that Charles was saying.

"Here." Charles handed the keys to Kevin. "I not

even bothering. But, when you dead don't blame me."

"Okay, I hear you. Now go before they leave you."

Kevin could feel the pain of betrayal riding his chest. It was a difficult pain to ignore.

"Just go!" Kevin said in a soft but demanding voice and Charles got up halfway and started running back to their vehicle. At that same time Kevin pushed against the police vehicle and ran into the bushes. He was sure to stay as low as possible.

He heard several shots fired from a distance in the bushes and then he heard rapid shots being fired in the area above. When he finally stopped and looked up, he saw the two police vehicles driving away. The officers who were sitting in the back were shooting into the bushes, in the direction where the ambush came from.

Kevin was certain that whoever was shooting at them didn't see when he ran into the bushes and this time he had a fair idea where he was.

He used the clear area above the road as his guide and he followed it for a distance. When he saw that he was approaching the village he made his way back up and remained just off the road.

He had recognized the houses, but there wasn't any stopping to rest this time. He kept walking until he reached the bus shed and he felt the excitement and relief move up into his chest when he saw the car, right where they'd left it.

He got into the car and made his way onto the highway and began heading to Wendell's house.

Kevin abandoned the vehicle in an empty lot and walked

through an open yard in order to get to Wendell's house without being seen. He saw Wendell mother's car parked in front this time and the gate was also open. He went into the yard where he listened to the voices of Wendell's mother and sister who were both talking in a nearby room. He couldn't make out exactly what they were saying.

He knocked on the door and waited. Karen asked who it was and when she didn't hear anyone answer, she came to the door within a few seconds. She was wearing a jeans and t-shirt and this time she had a surprised look on her face when she saw Kevin appear from the side of the house.

"Kevin! What you doing here?" she said with a worried look on her face and stared across her shoulders to see if anyone saw him come into their yard.

He was careful not to be seen.

"Kev, yuh face all over the news, why you still walking around like nothing happen? Come inside."

"No, I not staying long. Wendell here?"

She remained at the inside of the door, looking at him from the corner of her eyes.

"No, he not home. I not even sure where he is."

"Okay. But, when was the last time you did see him?"

"Earlier this morning, why?

"He might be in trouble, I need to see him. You have a number I could reach him on?"

"Oh God." Her expression changed immediately, and he noticed that she was starting to panic. "Yeah, you could reach him on his same number."

Kevin pierced his eyes at her, shocked by what she

just said. He gave her an opportunity to correct herself, but she didn't need to.

She stood there studying the sudden change in his face.

"What?" he said in a soft, angry voice.

Her face was confused.

He shook his head as he tried to cope with the instant feeling of betrayal. It was as if karma was already having its revenge. The anxiety and confusion were going to his head and he was beginning to feel as if he was about to explode.

He had tried calling Wendell's phone several times last night, hoping that he had purchased one, and now to find out this. Kevin clenched his fist. But, before he lost control of himself, he turned to walk away, hoping that he wouldn't place his anger on the wrong person.

It was like Wendell had completely changed. Kevin had no idea who he was anymore. First, he disappeared from the fight which was not like him, and then he lied about his phone being lost. Something wasn't adding up. There was no way Wendell could have changed so quickly without anyone noticing. He wasn't that smooth.

"What happen?" she asked.

Kevin could feel the pressure lingering in his head, confusing his thoughts. He had no idea what was going on and he hadn't made any plans. His intentions were plain and simple. He would come here and meet with Wendell and they'd both come together and retrieve the memory card. But, unfortunately for him, it was as if Wendell had something else on his agenda.

He took a deep breath and lifted his head, wishing

that he was the one who was overreacting and there would be an explanation. His shoulders and arms became tensed and he felt as if he didn't even know himself.

He opened his eyes and focused on the blue skies. It was a beautiful day. The type of day that would usually give him the feeling of comfort and a joy to be alive. But this time it was different. It made him realize that shit happens. In reality he was a fugitive. His time was becoming limited and there was definitely no room for sympathizing.

He turned and looked at her. She had no idea what was going on, or what was about to take place. But, one thing he knew for sure was that she'd never forgive him for what he was about to do.

Within a blink of an eye he dipped his hand beneath his jersey and pulled out the gun. Her eyes opened wide and she attempted to run. He grabbed her by her hand and hit her on her head with the gun butt. Her screams had been cut short and he pushed her inside and closed the door behind them.

Her mother came running out from somewhere in the back. She froze when she realized what was taking place.

"Where Jimmy?" Kevin said, keeping control of the situation.

"He in his bedroom," their mother answered.

"Let him come out here now!"

She called out to him and he answered and came out within some seconds. When he saw Kevin with the gun, he stopped at his mother's side and wrapped his arms around her.

Karen was on the ground holding her head and crying. There was blood between her fingers.

Kevin instructed everyone to sit on the couch, and they obeyed.

He wasn't proud of the way he had handled the situation, but he knew it was what he needed to do in order to get to the bottom of everything.

"I really didn't mean for any of this to happen, and I don't want nobody else to get hurt," he said, looking specifically at their mother. "But Wendell playing games and I need to find out what going on."

They all looked angry, except for Karen. She looked as though she was in a lot of pain.

Kevin reminded himself that the strategy was to show no sympathy.

"Hmm," their mother sighed and shook her head. "So that is what this is about? You standing in my living room and pointing a gun at we because you think Wendell playing games?"

"Okay, sorry," Kevin said. "I don't think. I know he playing games."

She was looking at him with disgust.

"Kevin?" She shook her head. "As a young man you really don't have no shame. You and Wendell is best friends for so much years. Allyuh use to laugh and make all kind of jokes right here in this house, and this is how you treating we? Look at Karen face! What she ever do to you?"

He looked at Karen and his conscience slowly began to resurface. He knew their mother was speaking the truth and he also knew he had no right to be carrying on the way he was. Regardless of those emotions, he comforted himself by believing it was his only choice.

After she said what she had to, he had no intentions of staying a minute longer than necessary.

"Karen…?"

She looked up at him. She wasn't crying, just holding her head and grimacing in pain.

"I need you to call Wendell and put the call on speaker. The faster you do that the better for everybody. You think you could do that?" he said and took the house phone to her without waiting for her to reply.

She hesitated and when he was about to repeat himself she took the phone from him and started dialing the number.

Wendell didn't answer on the first attempt and Kevin told her to try again.

This time he answered within the fourth ring.

"Hello."

She looked at Kevin and was handing the phone to him, but he signaled her to go along with the conversation before giving the phone to him.

"Yeah Wendell, what going on with you?"

There was a lot of breeze blowing into the phone and it gradually eased up and then he started talking again. "Yeah, everything alright. How come you still home? You not going class today?"

"Yeah. I leaving home in a little while."

"Oh, okay. Well I just have to make a spin and collect something before I come home, so I would see you when you get back home later, okay?"

"Alright, cool."

"What you wanted?"

She seemed confused by his question. She looked up at Kevin again. He was listening to the conversation while working out his approach. He was contemplating whether to confront him immediately or allow him to give his explanation.

"Kay?" Wendell called, sensing that something was wrong. She was still looking up at Kevin for further instructions.

"Kay?" Wendell called out to her in a more concerned voice.

Kevin took the phone and took it off speaker and walked away.

"Hey buddy, what going on?" Kevin said, trying to keep his cool. He was now a few steps away from where they were sitting.

"Who is this? Kevin?"

Kevin slowly nodded. Still angry and confused. "Yes… yeah, is me."

"Oh, okay. What going on?"

"Well, I trying to find out that same thing. How about, you tell me?"

There wasn't any hesitation coming from Wendell's end. "Well, I now went and check Steve and I on my way back up the road. I just have one more stop to make before coming home."

Kevin's eyes went to Wendell's family when he heard him mention coming home. He knew that wasn't going to be a good idea.

"Anyhow." Wendell's tone of voice changed from calm to hyper. "What going on with you and this news thing? I try calling you whole day yesterday and I wasn't getting you. I even pass and the place was in darkness."

While Wendell spoke, Kevin worked out his defence. One thing Wendell was good at was bullshitting people and as much as his story sound convincing, Kevin knew that the truth would be revealed once he was under pressure.

Kevin tightened his grip on the phone without realizing. He was becoming angry and frustrated of all the misinterpretations. During that time, he never took his eyes off of Wendell's family and he kept the gun pointing at them as a means of intimidation.

He took some slow breaths to remain calm. Wendell was quietly waiting for an answer and it was at that moment that Kevin decided that he'd go with the calm approach.

"I wasn't home yesterday. But that is not the point. I tried calling you so much times on this same number that you claim you lost."

"Don't even start that." Wendell was becoming angry. "Don't try to make me feel guilty about none of this. Just like how you going through yuh stress, I going through things too."

Kevin laughed at his selfish comparison. "What you going through?"

"Me, Steve and Sean lost a good friend too. Not only you."

"And that give you the right to act the way you acting?"

"How I acting?"

"You ignoring all my calls?"

"I ignoring all...? Hold on. Yeah, you could park right here." Kevin heard him say to someone in a low voice and then he heard when the car door closed. He listened carefully but the place was as quiet as before.

"I not ignoring nobody." Wendell was back on the phone. "I know how far we come from and what we went through so I would never do something like that. I didn't see any miss calls and that is the truth, and whenever I see you I will prove it." He was carrying on with no trace of stopping. "I tried calling you whole day yesterday and I even pass by yuh place. When you reach home you would see the miss calls. It wasn't my fault that you wasn't home. So stop blaming me."

Kevin had no idea how to respond. He walked to the dining table and pulled out the chair. The hand with the gun was stretched out on the table keeping his aim and his other hand was on his head in a thinking posture.

"You know what still bothering me? I thought you tell me you lost yuh phone in the scuffle?"

"Yes, that is where I lost it. I didn't lie about that. I have a new phone and I went and replaced the SIM card yesterday morning."

Kevin didn't know what else to ask. Wendell's story was believable. Kevin studied Wendell's family and realized that he might've been overacting and had even broken another rule in the process. They had once vowed to protect each other's family as they would protect their own. An apology would not be acceptable for what he had done to Wendell's sister.

They were quiet for a long while until Wendell asked if he was still there.

"Yeah, I right here," Kevin answered with tears running down his face. The guilt and frustration were too much to cope with.

"Bro, you wouldn't even believe half of the things I went through. I don't know what else to do or where to go from here. Right about now, I just feeling so lost. I could hardly think straight."

"Hmm, I really sorry to hear that. I wouldn't pretend, because I can't even start to imagine what you going through. But, just tell me what you want me to do, and I would do it."

Kevin was quiet. He was ashamed of what he had done, and he was afraid of what he was about to face out there.

"You want to wait and I would come and meet you there or something?"

"Nah, no… no." He shook his head. That was an easy decision. He looked at the bruises on Karen's face which was at the moment being attended to by her mother. He knew Wendell all too well, and if it was one thing. Wendell would definitely freak out when he saw his sister's face. And to make matters worse, he'd definitely go crazy when he finds out that she was attacked by one of his friends.

He would have to meet Wendell at another location and he must not find out what happened at his house. It would be a difficult and risky task. But, it was worth the try.

"You would have to meet me somewhere else. Most likely by ah abandon house or something. The police know we is friends and they would come here to look for me quicker than you think."

"Okay, that is true. You have anywhere in mind?"

Kevin started thinking.

"What about that old building on John Street?" Kevin said, in a low voice, so that Wendell's family wouldn't hear their arrangements.

"Which one? The one where all them homeless people does be? Or the one that burn down the other day?"

The one with the homeless persons was the closer of the two and Kevin would have to stay off of the road as best as he could, so he saw it as the better choice.

"Yeah, the one with the homeless people."

"Okay, and what time you want me to meet you there?"

He looked at the time on a clock on the living room wall. It was almost four o'clock. Time wasn't the problem though. He was thinking about the risk involved in leaving the house and the risk of staying there a minute longer. There wasn't much of a difference.

"Five o'clock good enough for you?" Kevin said.

There was a pause on Wendell's end.

"I might have to meet up with you a little later than that. I come to organize something for Steve and I don't know how long I would be here."

Kevin was curious. "Something like what?"

"Nah, he just ask me to collect something from somebody here and keep it for him."

Wendell was speaking in an unfamiliar code. Kevin was studying why Steve would ask Wendell to do anything for him after what he said, and if that was the case, why was it so important and confidential? Kevin's new objective was to make the arrangements and leave, so he left the question for when they met later on.

"Well we would meet up around six, six-thirty instead, okay?"

"Yeah, that will be plenty better." Wendell said.

"Okay. Well, six-thirty then."

"Alright, let me see how fast I could organize here and come and meet you."

"Okay, no problem." Kevin hung up and began anticipating his next move.

Karen's mother had finished cleaning up her face and they were all consoling each other on the couch, waiting to hear what else Kevin had in mind.

Kevin had to find a way to leave the house with the assurance that neither one of them would call Wendell and inform him of what had taken place.

He was staring at them and they were looking right back at him. He got up with his chair and took a seat in front of them like a teacher supervising his detention class.

"Okay, here what going on," Kevin started saying. "I have a little problem and I hope we could help each other out."

They were all paying attention. He waited a while and then took a deep breath before continuing.

"I make arrangements to meet Wendell this evening because this whole thing with me being on the news is a big setup. I see something that I not supposed to see. And, to make matters worse, the police is the ones behind it."

He was trying his best to reason with them. Though he wasn't sure if they were understanding or if they just wanted him to leave. He began explaining with more details.

"I have video evidence of the police controlling a drug house where people making cocaine. They even kill a few people in that video. I don't have the video on me now, but it in a safe place and I know that they not going to give up until they get it or until I dead… or both."

Their mother looked as though she was coming to terms what he was saying.

"I never mean for any of this to happen, and I real sorry. But I was scared and I didn't have nowhere else to go."

"Just tell me what you want Kevin?" Their mother interrupted in a lower voice than his. There was a hint of demand in her voice.

Kevin was surprised. He looked at her with a serious face and realized that she was willing to say or agree to anything in order for him to leave. He took a while before speaking.

"I don't want Wendell to find out what happened here today. I need him to help me figure out how I getting through this."

She shook her head and sweep her hand through the air, disregarding anything else he wanted to say.

"Okay."

"Okay?"

"Yes, okay. I understand and I would give you my word that he wouldn't find out about this. Just don't go and do anything stupid."

Kevin stood up. He kept his eyes on her and it was the first time she didn't look him in his face. He didn't believe a single word she said, and he wasn't going to take that risk. He had a better idea.

"I want Karen to drop me somewhere," he said.

Karen was startled. She started crying and pulled her mother closer to her. Her mother's expression made it obvious that she wasn't going to allow it to happen. She whispered something into Karen's ear and it calmed her down a little.

"You could take my car," her mother finally said. "Look the key on the cupboard over by the fridge." She pointed to it, but Kevin didn't move or look away. He despised the way Karen was acting towards him. He kept the gun pointing at them and ordered everyone to get up and go into their mother's room which was next to Wendell's bedroom in the back. They'd done so quietly.

As they sat on the bed Kevin had gone into the closet, taking out a few clothes and instructed Karen to tie her mother and brother's hands and feet. Karen and her brother started crying and pleading for mercy.

"Listen," he said calmly but neither one of them obeyed. They were being more dramatic than the situation called for and he was becoming annoyed.

"Listen!" Kevin said in a loud voice and they were both quiet and looking in his direction. Their hands were still clasped together in their silent plea for mercy.

"I going to drive myself. Just do what I say and let me get out from here."

Karen studied his face and then complied. When she was finished, Kevin tied her up and covered their mouths in such a way that it would be difficult and somewhat painful if they attempted to scream or speak. Their mother was then left in her room and they were both dragged to their individual rooms and he locked each door.

To him it was a cruel act, but he knew it was the only assurance he'd have of keeping them quiet. Hopefully they would be found sometime during the night after he met with Wendell.

Kevin went into the kitchen where he took the keys for the car. He then locked up the house and left.

CHAPTER ELEVEN

The abandoned house that they had spoken of was only ten minutes drive from Wendell's house, but Kevin thought it would be wiser to park at another location and walk across when it was closer to the time they had arranged to meet.

He had thought about going home and retrieving the memory card, but decided not to.

At five o'clock he became impatient and left the car at the car park of a grocery store and walked over to the house.

The house was a two-storey building with broken windows and open doors. The lawn had not been maintained over the years and the grass was as high as five feet in some parts of the yard. Kevin had heard that the owners had migrated almost six years ago, and homeless persons were the only ones who'd occupied the house. But they would mostly use it as a safe zone when they were ready to get high and for sleeping.

Kevin squeezed through the front gate, having to

push against the tall grass that was blocking it, and made his way along the overgrown footpath and went into the house. The place was dark; he heard a rustling and cooing from the pigeons that lived in the ceiling. The rooms stank with bird shit.

From the look of the place it was obvious that most of the activities took place in the room he was standing in. There Cardboard boxes lay on the floor like beds and ragged clothes were used as the bedspread.

Breathing as shallowly as possible, Kevin quickly made his way upstairs to a room in the back. When he got there, he opened the windows and breathed in the fresh air. To his left, the sun was sinking on the horizon in an orange glow.

Kevin thought that this might very well be the last sunset he would ever see.

He kept himself hidden behind the window until the sun sank, and the place became dark.

The quietness in the room was becoming overwhelming and it made Kevin think of the different ways things could turn out and the fear of being imprisoned overcome him once more. He dreaded the thought of being away from Shantel, forcing her to raise their child on her own.

It was 6:55 p.m. and there still wasn't any sign of Wendell. A short time after Kevin heard the front door open. He listened carefully but nothing else was heard beside the noise coming from the birds. He walked to the door hoping that he'd be in a better position to see who had entered the house or what was taking place. From where he was standing he could hear someone coming up the stairs and then he saw their shadow. The place was too dark to see if it was Wendell.

Kevin took a step back and picked up an iron pipe that was lying on the ground. He held it in a firm grip prepared to use it if he had to. He would only use the firearm if things got out of hand since the gunshot would draw unnecessary attention.

He waited for the shadow.

"Kevin...?"

He heard Wendell calling his name in a low voice and saw him walking pass the room.

"Kev..."

Kevin pulled opened the door before Wendell could finish saying his name and signaled him to come into the room. As soon as he entered the room, he'd gone to the window and started coughing and breathing heavily. Kevin shook his head. Wendell always had a way to make a problem seem a lot bigger than it was.

"How the hell you making out in here?" Wendell asked without turning and looking at him. Kevin didn't answer. He waited and when Wendell had gotten enough fresh air and turned to him, Kevin looked at the time on his watch. Wendell noticed.

"I tried my best to reach earlier, but I couldn't help it. The ball wasn't in my court." He looked genuinely disappointed.

"Yeah, no problem. I figured that much. What you had to do for Steve anyway?"

Wendell was looking at him straight in his face. "Remember the deal he had with Patrick?"

Kevin remembered immediately. Patrick was the person who Steve would get his drugs from. He supplied most of the drug blocks in central with the highest grade of marijuana, and he also sold cocaine. After stealing the drugs from Biggs, Steve contacted Patrick and made arrangements for him to purchase the drugs at a very low price. Steve had never dealt with cocaine and had no intentions to, so it was an easy decision for him.

"Yeah," Kevin answered. "What happen to him?"

"Steve wanted me to go there and let him know that the deal was still on, and because of the situation he would make arrangements to sell it at a later date."

Kevin realized that Steve had trusted Wendell to pass the message but not to make the deal. It was obvious that he wasn't ready to put all his trust in him.

"Okay, but why Steve didn't just make you handle it for him?" Kevin asked in order to know if Wendell understood that the amount of trust Steve once had for him wasn't there anymore.

Wendell thought about it. "You know how Steve is. When so much money involved, he does rather do these kind of things for himself."

It was true, but it wasn't the answer Kevin was looking for, but it would have to work for now.

"And what Patrick say?"

"He didn't have a problem with it. You know how he is. He business always running."

"Yeah, for real. But how you take so long?"

"I had a little wait and then it had a lot of traffic."

"Okay."

They were both quiet for a while. Kevin was thinking. He knew a lot of time had passed and although he was ready for them to start working out a strategy, he didn't want it to look as though he was only concerned with himself.

"How the funeral pass?"

"Hmm, well like any other funeral. With crying and screaming, and people wishing they had the power to raise the dead."

Wendell walked across to the window with a saddened look on his face. They didn't say anything to each other for almost five minutes.

"What happen?" Kevin said.

Wendell didn't budge, and Kevin repeated the question.

He shook his head. "Nothing." He turned to Kevin. "Imagine almost two weeks done pass, and he bury just yesterday and is like I still can't believe he really gone."

Kevin could understand Wendell's pain. He didn't have to be at the funeral to be depressed by the reality of losing someone close. He was only nine years old when both his parents died in a car accident and his grandmother took him and his brother in. She had gotten a stroke and passed away a year later when he was sixteen, forcing him and his brother to face the harsh reality. They both began working and eventually they'd gone their separate ways. He remembered the pain and stood there quietly, giving Wendell all the time he needed.

Wendell folded his hands and took a few more minutes, keeping his eyes outside the window.

"Is just how you could never tell what will happen," Wendell said, breaking the silence. Kevin didn't say anything.

"It had me thinking though. And I come to realize

that we does actually cause we own problems." He turned and looked at Kevin again. "If we did never do all those things in the past, and if we didn't take them drugs from Biggs we would've never be in this position today. Maybe everything would've turn out different." He paused for a few seconds and turned his head back to whatever he was looking at outside the window.

"What you think?" he said.

Kevin thought about it. He knew it wasn't something he needed to think about, but to him it came across as though Wendell was making a suggestion rather than asking a question.

Wendell looked at him when he didn't get an answer.

"Yeah, that is true," Kevin finally answered.

"Hmm, I glad you agree with me. Because I have a feeling it eh finish yet." Wendell shook his head and Kevin noticed him clenching his jaw.

"I have something to tell you, Wendell continued. "But I would do that after you say what you have to say."

Kevin was studying what he could possibly have to tell him that wasn't more important to him than what he was about to hear. Nevertheless, Kevin wasn't going to allow that to distract him at the moment. He gathered his thoughts and started telling Wendell everything that had happened, from the moment he'd escaped Biggs to the moment his face was seen on the news while he was at the hospital and then being hunted down by officers.

But he didn't mention his conversation with Steve and that he had gone back to the hideout.

It took Kevin a little over two hours to tell his story.

They were both sitting side by side on the window sill

when he had finished.

Wendell sighed and stood up, slowly brushing his hands through his hair as if he had just inherited the world of problems.

"So, what now?" he asked.

"Well, that is what I want you to help me figure out."

Wendell was thinking. "Well it not sounding like it will make much of a difference if they get back the memory card or not. They might still find that you see and hear too much."

"Exactly…"

"What about if you show it to somebody big in the business? Somebody bigger than this whole operation?"

Kevin joined him on his feet. "Yeah, that might work. But, somebody like who?"

"Well that is where we would have to do we own research."

"Yeah, but remember I can't move around too much. So, basically I really need yuh help to get out of this one."

"Yeah, don't worry yourself, I not planning to do anything else."

"Okay, thanks, I really appreciate that."

Kevin felt relieved.

"Well we will have to find somewhere safe for you to hide out while we work this out," said Wendell.

Kevin was wondering where exactly he might have in mind, and he was hoping that Wendell wouldn't suggest somewhere that he would feel uncomfortable staying or would have to have interactions with anyone from his family after what had taken place earlier.

"You went to the hideout since?" asked Wendell.

"No. Why?" Kevin said, hoping that it wouldn't be one of Wendell's suggestions.

"What about there?"

Kevin shook his head. "Nah, I find it too far away from everything. I would rather stay somewhere that I could monitor what going on in the news and if I have to move or contact anybody I wouldn't have any problem."

"Oh, okay. And you wouldn't want to stay by my house?"

"Nah, I done tell you already that, that would be too risky. And I don't want to get your family mix up in all this."

"Well, the only other place I could think about right now, is right here."

"Hmm." Kevin moved his eyes around the room and his focus remained on the unsecured door. It was his biggest concern, especially knowing how badly he needed to rest and he would not be able to sleep comfortably without wondering if someone would come into the room while he was asleep.

"So, what you think?"

Kevin looked back at Wendell. He was glad to be distracted although he wasn't given enough time to think it through. He took another obvious glance before giving him an answer.

"Yeah, well. It not that bad and I done here already." He sat on the window sill. "But I don't have anything to sleep on, or anything to eat. So that is the next problem."

"Nah, don't worry about that. I will organize them things and bring them back."

"Okay, cool. Thanks."

"Yeah, no problem, don't worry about it."

Wendell looked at the time on his watch and then looked out the window observing the number of people who were at the grocery store across the street. "I will go and get some things for you now. I wouldn't be long."

"Okay," Kevin said.

Kevin remained sitting at the window a little longer, trying to figure out a way to retrieve the memory card from his apartment without being caught. None of his ideas felt one hundred percent safe.

After about forty-five minutes of being alone Kevin heard a noise coming from downstairs. It sounded like bags and boxes being dragged across the room. He could also hear male and female voices. Kevin went to the door, peeping through a crack he'd made by slightly opening the door.

He noticed that the front door was open and that created enough light for him to see that there were three men and two women. They were all dressed in ragged clothing and two of the men were bringing in a large box. One of the women was dragging a garbage bag to a corner of the room. She then ripped it open, spilling the rubbish inside.

After getting the box inside, both men along with the two persons who were waiting around took it apart and made five beds with the use of additional boxes from within the room. They were made of similar lengths and stacked at a specific height to protect them from the cold ground.

When they were finished they gathered around the

woman with the bag and helped themselves to whatever they found to eat.

After eating they took some time to share a needle before closing the door and making the place dark again. Only their voices were heard as they slowly welcomed the silence.

Kevin had no intentions of disturbing them. He knew they would be aware of his presence when Wendell returned.

He carefully closed the door and went back to the window, this time sitting on the ground and keeping his eyes in the direction of the door.

His pains were obvious. Moving around wasn't as painful as a few days ago, but it was excruciating to put his body in certain positions. He tried his best to ignore the pain as much as he could.

His eyes were closing. He knew it was important to stay awake to ensure his safety, but he also knew it would be a matter of time before he fell asleep.

CHAPTER TWELVE

"Kevin? Kev, wake up!"

Kevin opened his eyes, panic coiling like a snake in his stomach. He threw his body on the ground, away from the person kneeling down beside him, before realizing that it was only Wendell. He placed his hand on his chest and started to take some deep breaths.

Wendell stood up and gave him a few more minutes before apologizing for startling him.

"Yeah, okay, small thing," Kevin said. He got back in a sitting position in an attempt to relax.

As his eyes wandered around the room he saw a few flattened cardboard boxes in one corner covered with a blanket of newspapers. There were two grocery bags on top.

When his heart had slowed to a normal beat, Kevin went across to the bags. He took a seat on the newspapers and it was only then that he remembered the homeless persons downstairs.

"Where you pass to reach upstairs?" Kevin said.

"Through the front door, why?" Wendell replied.

"Nah, I did hear some talking downstairs earlier, so I thought them people was still downstairs."

"Yeah, right there I pass. But them not studying me."

"Oh, okay."

Kevin began looking through the bags. He found water, juice, bread and some other items. He made himself a quick sausage sandwich while Wendell sat quietly at the window. Only after he took his last bite did he look at his watch. His eyes widened in shock.

"Is eleven-thirty-seven," he said.

"Yeah? said Wendell.

"But…" Kevin began, then stopped.

"What?" Wendell said.

"Nothing."

But Kevin was suspicious once again that Wendell had taken much longer than he should have.

"Something wrong?" Wendell asked.

Kevin shook his head. "Nah, I didn't realize it was so late."

"Oh, okay." Wendell paused. "I didn't have any money on me so I had to pass home for some."

"Okay." Kevin took out two more slices of bread and opened the tab on another can of Vienna sausages. He was confused as to why Wendell was acting normal after going home. He then began to weigh the possibility of him not finding his mother or Karen and Jimmy. He was looking at Wendell from the corner of his eyes to see if he would notice any change in his mood. But Wendell seemed preoccupied.

"How yuh mother and them going?"

"Good, I hope. They wasn't home. Normally Jimmy

does go by the park with my mother and make some laps around the savannah. And around that time Karen woulda still be in class."

"Oh, okay. So, they wasn't in their room either?"

"Nah. The rooms was empty."

"Okay. And how come you didn't try calling them?" Kevin asked. He wanted to cover all angles.

"Nah, my phone have to charge. Plus, them is big people. I not worried.

"Alright, true. But that weird though. When I was there earlier yuh sister was organizing for class, and I really think I did hear yuh mother them say something about going to the savannah."

"Yeah, I wouldn't doubt it."

"Well, you know how yuh mother could be sometimes."

"Don't remind me." Wendell had a grin on his face.

Kevin was glad that it had went smoothly. He had finished eating and he placed the garbage in one of the bags and put it at the foot of the cardboard bed.

Wendell stood up with his hands folded across his chest. His grin had vanished, and he was now grim.

Kevin had seen that look before.

He looked up at Wendell and shook his head, preparing his mind for the worst.

"What happen now?" he asked

Wendell didn't answer at once. He looked as if he was trying to form his words as best as possible. Almost a minute passed before he started talking.

"When I was home I happen to catch the ten o'clock news." Wendell paused for a few seconds. He was looking straight at Kevin's face.

Kevin was anxious to know what the officers had come up with this time.

"Yeah, and, what they saying now?"

"Well..." He was studying something. "They place a reward for anybody who bring you in."

Kevin looked around the room, the piece of iron was on the far side of the room next to the door. He realized that he'd have no other choice but to use the gun to defend himself if Wendell decided to betray him for the love of money. He hoped that wasn't the case.

"How much is the reward?" Kevin asked.

"Fifty thousand," Wendell said after hesitating for a few seconds.

"Hmm, that is plenty money."

"I know."

Kevin didn't have any idea what to do or say. As much as he knew it wasn't possible, he wished he'd just disappear, just like that, in thin air. Wendell was just standing there with his hands still folded across his chest as if he was contemplating on whether he should accept the money or not. Or maybe he was thinking about what he had done at the club and what he was about to do.

For some reason Kevin felt as if Wendell was telling him that he had sold him out for the money. He was thinking of a way to talk him out of it. Money changes everything, but their friendship was something to think about, and it was worth a try.

"So, what you decide to do?" Kevin finally asked the question. Wendell looked surprised.

"What you mean?"

"You know what I mean. What we going to do now?"

Wendell screwed up his face. "Well, this turning out to be harder than I thought. Knowing that so much money involve, plenty people would be looking for you. And it going to be so much harder for you to move around and you wouldn't be able to stay one place for too long either."

Kevin let out a long breath. He was both relieved and surprised that Wendell was still on his side. Nonetheless he was somewhat embarrassed of the fact that his experiences had him nervous and it was also giving him trust issues.

"What about the memory card?" Wendell asked.

"What about it?"

"You make any copies yet?"

"No."

"Okay, well we will have to make some copies. The more we make the better."

"Alright, no problem."

"Okay, well you could stay here and I will go and get the memory card and make the copies."

Kevin lowered his eyes. He wanted to remain involved as much as possible. Kevin knew that his survival and clearing his name was depending on the evidence on that card. Retrieving it was most important to him and he felt as if he was the only person who would be willing to protect it with their life.

"I think it would be better if I go with you. We can get it and from there we would go and make the copies," Kevin said.

"You really want to take that risk? It have plenty

police outside there. I could go and get it now and make the copies and reach back here before morning. They wouldn't even suspect anything."

His plan sounded tempting, but Kevin's trust in people and their words wasn't the same as before. He had to convince Wendell and tag along.

"Nah, it have some other things I have to collect. So I would go and get them stuff one time."

Wendell was looking at him as if he was trying to get into his head. Kevin turned and started walking to the door.

"Wait," Wendell said, gesturing for him to remain. "Let me go and make sure everything safe in the area and around yuh house before you go outside. When I went out earlier it had plenty officers patrolling, that is why I tell you I woulda go and handle it. I not too sure how things looking now."

Kevin sat down. "Yeah, that is a good idea," he agreed.

"Okay, so you could go ahead and take a rest and I would go and do the same and I would make sure everything okay by your place before I come across here in the morning, okay?"

Kevin looked at him with a concerned face. He was becoming worried that their arrangements would be compromised if Wendell went home to his family.

"So, you going home and wait?"

"Nah." Wendell said without hesitating. He had an, obviously not look on his face. "I not going back home to get them mix up in all this. I would go and spend the night by Curtis them and go home tomorrow once everything work out."

"Or, okay, cool." Kevin felt relieved.

Curtis was Wendell's cousin and he lived two streets from Kevin's apartment. Regardless of the situation with Wendell's family, that was no doubt the better decision.

It was a fact that time was against them, but he knew it would be a lot safer to move around while the place was still in darkness. Tonight was out of the question since Kevin was feeling very weak due to lack of sleep, but tomorrow night or perhaps the early part of the morning would be more suitable.

Wendell said he would be back at 4:30 in the morning, which was only a few hours away.

"You sure that would be enough time for you?" he asked. "Cause you look like you would need all the sleep you could get."

"Nah, I good. That is enough time." Kevin rubbed his face, trying to look more awake. It didn't make much difference.

"I will have enough time to sleep when all of this over," he said.

"Okay, well you go ahead and get some rest. I will come back and meet you in a little while."

Wendell left, and Kevin lay down on the newspapers, looking up to the ceiling. It didn't take him long to fall asleep.

CHAPTER THIRTEEN

Wendell returned around 4 a.m. bringing a change of clothes for Kevin. Kevin was still asleep, but got up when Wendell entered the room. He dressed quickly. Wendell had brought a hoodie, but Kevin didn't pull it over his head since that might have drawn attention at that hour of the morning. But the coldness outside still made him shiver even in the short walk from the house to the car parked outside the gate.

Wendell got in and started the engine and took the shortest route to Kevin's place.

There were a lot of police vehicles patrolling the area. The bright blue flashing lights were easily seen from a distance. It made Kevin uneasy at first, but Wendell kept assuring him that everything was going to be okay.

After driving for few minutes Wendell made a left turn and then drove about one hundred metres before pulling up in front of Kevin's apartment. There weren't any officers or vehicles seen on his street. Kevin found this strange—he was certain he would have to sneak into his place—but he kept his thoughts to himself.

"Hold this." Wendell handed a cell phone to him. It was already on. Kevin noticed this after he'd pressed a random button and the screen lighted up.

"It will look suspicious if I stay here. I will park on another street and you will give me ah call when you get yuh stuff, okay?"

Kevin nodded. "Yeah, alright, no problem." He opened the door and got out.

Wendell quickly drove away without wasting any time.

Kevin walked towards the house. His apartment was the only one with all its lights off. He inspected the front door and only opened it when he was satisfied that there wasn't any forced entry. He locked the door behind him.

As his eyes adjusted to the darkness he was in disbelief of what he saw. Inside the house was ransacked and the couch was ripped up and pushed across the room. His radio, DVD player, TV and all his CD's where scattered on the floor as if the country had been hit by an earthquake. The entire place was a mess.

Beyond the living room area, he could see his kitchen appliances on the floor together with broken plates and glasses. It was evident that whoever broke into his place had destroyed his furniture and appliances, apparently out of sheer anger.

Kevin got on his toes and walked through the rubble making his way to his bedroom.

As he pushed open the door he noticed that his bed was lifted and leaning against the wall and all of his clothes were torn up and scattered across the room.

The window curtains were pulled down making it

possible for everyone to see inside the house. It was something that he should have noticed before entering, and he cursed himself in his mind.

He went back into the living room and retrieved one of the table chairs. He placed it below the ceiling tile that he had marked and climbed up.

He pushed on the ceiling and the memory card and chain that he'd hidden fell to the ground. He picked up the memory card and stuck it into his pocket. He studied the chain and realized that because of his situation, finding a sale for it wasn't important right now. He left it there.

While standing on the chair Kevin noticed the neighbour who lived two houses down the street leaving his house for an early morning jog. It was something he'd normally do around this time on random days of the week.

Kevin put the ceiling back into place and came off the chair before the man saw him.

He knew that staying in the house longer than necessary would be too risky. He took out the cell phone and began dialing Wendell's number.

"Yeah, you get everything?" Wendell answered on the first ring.

"Yeah, I have everything. You could come and pick me up now."

"Alright, no problem, I coming."

Kevin hung up and stuck the phone back into his pocket. He stood at the bedroom door studying the damage done to the place. Throughout the week he was thinking to himself that he would return home when everything was over and focus on building back his life and his relationship with Shantel. But now after seeing the state of the house, he realized it would not be so straightforward.

He saw a flash of blue light in the wall mirror that almost instantly disappeared. He turned and walked to the window.

Outside he could see several police cars coming in his direction at a fast pace. They had only their headlights on.

Kevin immediately dropped on his hands and knees and crawled into the bathroom. He knew there was a fifty-fifty chance of escaping, so his first priority was to hide the memory card again.

He got on his feet and started looking around. There were too many things going through his mind making it very difficult for him to think. As much as he tried to focus he couldn't think of anywhere to hide it. The ceiling was too high and besides the fact that the toilet contained water, it was something that they'd easily break apart in their search.

He pushed the shower curtain aside and stared at the tiled walls in frustration as if there was once a secret passageway.

He could hear footsteps moving around the house now. They were closer than he thought and yet he was still holding the memory card.

Within a few seconds he heard the doorknob shaking. He clenched his fists and started pacing back and forth. He was confused and overcome by anxiety. He held his fist to his head, hoping to come up with something before they came running in.

He held onto the curtain rod and attempted to

reach the ceiling. It was no use. He also thought about unscrewing the curtain rod to move the ceiling tile, but he knew it would be difficult to put the ceiling back into place as if it was never tampered with. It was then that he came up with a brilliant idea.

He unscrewed the curtain rod and stuck the memory card in. He screwed it back and crawled back into the bedroom and got behind the bed. It was then that he felt and remembered that the gun was still stuck in his waist. He pulled it out and slid it across the room. It hit the wall and went behind the wardrobe.

He had no use for a firearm there. His shooting skills would never overpower theirs. And, besides, his motive wasn't not getting caught, but not being killed. His plan was to remain there until they found him.

Within a few moments the front door was opened and he could hear their light footsteps. It sounded like four persons or more. They were whispering to each other as they moved throughout the rooms. No one had yet entered the bedroom.

Kevin made himself smaller and prepared himself to take yet another beating. It was like a norm that had been fitted into their portfolio. He knew it was something he couldn't get away from.

He heard their footsteps entered the room. They moved towards the window and after a few moments he heard someone take up the chain.

"He was here," one of officers said to another in a low voice.

"Yeah, the bitch was actually telling the truth," another one replied and then they were all quiet for a while.

The phone started vibrating in Kevin's pocket and as soon as he held it down to ease the vibration it started to ring.

"Fellas, he behind the bed!" one of the officer shouted and the bed was immediately pulled to the ground. As Kevin looked up he saw three masked officers with guns pointing at his face. Two more officers came running into the room and all five guns were pointing at him.

"Get up," one of the officers said and pulled Kevin up by his arm. Kevin was on his feet without even realizing it. Another officer held on to his free arm and they both took him into the living room, kicking aside whatever was in their way. They'd put him to sit on one of the dining table chairs.

"You call him yet?" the officer who was doing all the talking said, and upon getting a negative response he lifted the radio to his mouth and communicated with someone by telling them that he had the suspect in custody.

After he had finished talking an officer came from outside with a roll of caution tape. He simply moved aside and gestured for the officer to proceed, and then the officer with the help of another used the tape and started wrapping it around Kevin's body, making sure to keep both of his hands behind his back. Kevin sat there and allowed them to do what they had to without resisting or attempting to negotiate. He knew that there was someone bigger than them who was in charge and calling the shots. That person was the decision maker and regardless of his plea for them to have mercy on him, that person was the only one who would give a listening ear. That was the person they were waiting for.

When they were finished with the tape Kevin could hardly move his hands. All the movements were lost from his wrist upward and he could also feel a tightness around his chest that made it even more difficult for him to breathe. He tried to ignore the discomfort, hoping that it would not become life threatening.

He looked around at the officers. There were six of them standing around in front of him. Their faces were hidden beneath ski masks.

None of the officers said anything after the call. They just held their positions, alertly holding their firearms in their hands.

They left the door open and Kevin was distracted by the blue flashing lights that were just turned on. Beyond the lights he saw that the sky was becoming bright. The sun hadn't yet appeared, but he could see its glare behind the clouds in the horizon.

The neighbourhood cars were starting to make their way through the street. Kevin noticed that a few of them were slowing down just enough to get a glimpse of what was taking place inside. It was only then that Kevin realized that the officer had intentionally made it difficult for them to see by turning on the lights.

Kevin leaned back on the chair in an attempt to take some of the tension off his chest. He exhaled and then relaxed. His twisting and turning actually made a difference.

The sun had come up and the leading officer signaled two officers to join him on the outside. Four of them remained inside, surrounding Kevin by positioning themselves at the four corners of the room. It was easy to see their eyes now. He also noticed that the officer standing to his left had a bullseye tattoo on his neck. It was the size of a walnut and looked as if it was professionally done. It wasn't customary to see tattoos on exposed parts of an officer's skin, so Kevin thought he looked more like a thug than an officer.

About ten minutes after Kevin heard a vehicle pull up and he heard the officers outside saying something just before seeing a few shadows approaching the door. Both officers in front of him straightened up and waited for the person to enter. Their anticipation made Kevin anxious.

"Good day, sir," the two officers said, almost simultaneously as they saluted a stocky built man neatly dressed in a khaki suit. He was wearing sunglasses and, oddly, holding a staff in his right hand. Kevin had no idea of police ranks, but he saw several badges on the man's chest and thought that he had to be a high person in the Police Service. The man gestured for both officers to relax and the officer who had done all the talking came in behind him and closed the door.

The man in the khaki suit walked closer to Kevin, observing him thoroughly.

"So, this is the fella who causing we all this trouble?" he said to no one in particular. It wasn't necessary for him to talk loudly due to the quietness and the closeness of everyone in the room. No one said anything. He remained quiet for a while as he continued observing Kevin's appearance.

"You have something for me?" the man said to Kevin. Kevin hesitated, though he knew very well that he was speaking about the memory card.

Kevin was thinking about the dangers of cooperating and whether he'd be able to walk out of there alive once he gave him what he wanted.

There was no telling who to trust anymore. Words had no meaning in these types of circumstances. Kevin wanted to be released and freed of all threats and slander to his name. The only thing he had on his mind was to stop hanging out with bad company and to walk the street and live a normal life. That was all he was thinking about before the man arrived. He thought about it so much that he hadn't taken the time to work out the steps of how he was planning to negotiate his freedom.

The man in the khaki suit looked around at them when he hadn't gotten an answer from Kevin.

"Like I talking to myself?" he said to the officers. He was obviously annoyed.

"Okay." He took a deep breath. "Let me start over." He took off his glasses and kept it in his hand. His eyes were black and cold, like a snake's.

"Let me tell you who I am. I is the man who tell these men what to do," he said. "My name not important. You know why? Because names only important for birth and death certificates." He paused. "I is a fair person. Well, at least, I would like to believe that." He smiled and looked around at his officers. They grinned back under their ski masks.

"So when I hear somebody come to my place of business looking for safety, and I gave the instructions that they should be protected and safely escorted out of there to reunite with their family. And that same person take something valuable to me, and on top of that they try to kill my people. I does get upset." He folded his arms and fixed his cold eyes on Kevin.

"Now you tell me. If you was me how you would've dealt with that?" His hands went behind his back and he turned and walked towards the kitchen, carefully stepping across the rubble.

"I waiting for yuh answer. Think fast because we don't have too much time. We have other criminal duties to perform." He was in the kitchen.

Kevin was thinking about a good enough answer. He had to do this under the intimidating stares coming from all the officers in the room.

"You have bottle water in this fridge?" The chief said while looking through the fridge.

"Yeah, it supposed to have some on the bottom shelf," Kevin said, hoping that the persons who had vandalized his place hadn't drank all of it.

"Okay good, I see it."

He came back into the living room and threw a bottle of water for each of his officers, who caught them easily without letting go of their guns.

"So?" He stood with his hands folded across his chest again, waiting for his answer.

"I woulda tell my officers to go and get it back," Kevin said, knowing that was what he wanted to hear.

"Good." He was nodding and smiling. "I like that answer. What about if they don't find it? What you would've done then?"

"I would go and try to find it for myself."

He continued nodding, and then the smile vanished from his face as quickly as a snake's flicking tongue. He closed his fist and punched Kevin in the stomach in one quick movement. Kevin felt all the air escape from his lungs and his eyes and mouth opened wide.

"Look I right here! Where my fucking memory card?" he said, his voice suddenly full of rage and the three officers instantly raised their machine guns to Kevin's face. Kevin tried his best to catch his breath and regain his focus, hoping not to pass out.

The chief definitely wasn't on games or any sort of runaround. He wanted an exact location of the memory card and Kevin knew wherever he directed him to, it had better be there.

Kevin started thinking whether he should give in or not. He didn't expect things to move from bad to worse this fast, and now he had limited time to come up with a good enough answer, or at least try to buy some time while he thought about it.

The chief was waiting. Kevin could see the anger in his face as he was becoming more and more impatient.

"I really don't want to disappoint you," Kevin said in a weak voice. He tried coughing to soothe the pain.

"What?" the chief said.

Kevin cleared his throat before repeating himself. "I don't want to disappoint you."

"What you mean by that?"

Kevin's mouth was trembling in fear and when the chief noticed that he gestured for his men to lower their guns.

Kevin's intention was to buy time and hopefully get some answers while he tried to change the chief's mood and persuade the chief to release him, so he could cause a diversion.

"How you know I was here?"

"What?" The chief seemed confused by the question."

"How you…"

"No," he interrupted. "I hear what you say. But what that have to do with anything?" He was still angry.

"Everything…"

"Hmm." He wiped his hand across his face, looking as though his frustration had reached its highest point. Kevin knew he'd have to continue talking without any hesitation, even if the chief wasn't paying attention.

"We does just know things," he said and looked at the others as though he was wondering how the question was connected to his purpose for being there. They were all looking at him as if they were disappointed that he was even tolerating the conversation. Kevin had him right where he wanted him. All he'd have to do was continue talking.

"I know it can't be that." Kevin shook his head in a negative way. "Police doesn't know these kind of things. Allyuh can't even solve the simplest crime."

The chief looked concerned and somewhat humiliated by the statement. "Look, right now you wasting my time. What you really trying to say?"

"Is not what I trying to say. Is what I saying."

"Okay, well, what you saying?"

"That I know you have an informant. You have somebody who tell you I was here."

The chief was studying. "I don't know what you talking about, but go ahead, I listening. And I really hope you making a point, because I don't like people to waste my time. Time is expensive."

"But somebody already waste yuh time without you even realizing it."

The chief looked around at his officers. They were all paying attention now.

"Listen, whatever you trying to say, stop fucking mumbling and just go ahead and say it," the chief said. "Because I really losing my patience here."

"Okay." Kevin pretended to give in. "I don't have the memory card," he said.

"Okay. So where it is? Who have it?"

"Yuh source."

"Hmm," He smiled in a psychotic way and shook his head, expressing his frustration. "And who you think is my source?"

Kevin had a fair idea that Wendell was the one who'd sold him out. It was a fifty-fifty assumption, but whether or not it was true he had no doubt that the chief was communicating with someone and whoever it was they'd have to be in contact with Wendell in order for Wendell to lead him here and then bring the police soon after.

Kevin knew they'd already captured him and if he'd have to die here at least he'd have an idea of the person who had sold him out. He needed to get to the bottom of this once and for all and separate his friends from his enemies.

"Your source. The person who bring me here and then you."

The chief started thinking. Kevin could tell that he was getting somewhere. The place was quiet for a while and the chief was in deep concentration.

"And if I tell you I don't believe nothing that you

saying right now?"

"Then you will find out sooner or later. Maybe after you kill me and you still see the video on the news, then you would realize that I was telling the truth all the time."

He gave Kevin a long hard stare and then he went to the talking officer and they were quietly conversing for a short while. He came back to Kevin afterwards.

"Okay, so I decide that I don't have nothing to lose. So, yeah, I have my source. But, even if I bring him here and I realize you lying, I would simply kill two of allyuh and still have ah good night sleep. This is what I do for a living. So hear what. I would give you one last chance and if you decide to stick to that story, I would do the needful."

He was waiting for an answer, but Kevin remained quiet, sticking to what he'd told him.

"Okay." He took a deep breath and took out his phone and made a call.

"Yeah, I hearing something else here. Search that fella for the memory card and if you don't find it, do whatever you have to do to get some answers. You have five minutes." The chief hung up and waited five minutes and then called back.

"Talk to me." There was a pause. "Okay, whatever," said the chief. "One of them lying. Bring him inside."

The door opened a short time after and Kevin waited anxiously to see who it was.

Tears started to run down his face as he saw Wendell being escorted inside and left to stand at the chief's side. His face was bruised, and his mouth was bleeding.

The chief looked at Wendell and then looked at

Kevin with only one thing on his mind.

"So, boss man?" the chief said to Wendell. "I hear you have something for me?" his voice was sounding very harsh. Wendell looked him in his face obviously clueless about what he was talking about. Kevin had no idea how this would turn out.

"What is that, boss?" His voice was sounding hoarse.

"Hmm…" the chief walked and took his glasses from the officer and put it on and then took his staff from the other officer. Kevin noticed when he'd tightened his grip on the lower end of the staff as if he was holding a golf club. As soon as he did that he swung around and dealt Wendell a blow to the side of his head. Wendell fell to the ground holding his head and groaning in pain. Kevin could see blood running down his face and on his hands. Blood was also dripping on the ground.

Kevin felt the muscles in his stomach lock as if he was getting a cramp.

The chief seemed very angry and Kevin had no idea if he'd receive the same treatment without a warning. He knew that the blows he had gotten in his stomach earlier was nothing compared to what he had just saw. And with his hands being tied, he couldn't imagine the level of pain he would have to bear. He would surely faint this time.

The chief wiped off the blood from his staff on Wendell's clothing.

"Get up!" he said to Wendell. He was still holding his head and groaning in pain. The chief then kicked him in his stomach causing him to roll over on his side. He moved his hands to his stomach and that was when Kevin saw his head. Kevin turned away on seeing Wendell's fractured skull. The cramping feeling in his stomach returned and this time it felt as if it was trying to force out his last meal. He felt a lump in his throat that was difficult to swallow. He couldn't look in Wendell's direction.

"Get up!" the chief snarled.

Kevin heard the officers moving behind him and that was when he turned around to see what was happening. He was afraid that it was him they were approaching.

Both officers walked over to Wendell and held him by his arms and brought him to his feet. He was weak, and he could hardly stand on his own.

Kevin kept himself together this time. He was too afraid to turn away.

Wendell's head and the front of his jersey was covered in blood and he was crying now and pleading for mercy.

"Where you hiding the memory card?"

Wendell shook his head. "I don't know," he said in a weak voice. The chief looked at Kevin.

There was that place in Kevin's mind that made him feel sorry for the way things were turning out, but he also knew there was a strong possibility that it was Wendell who had them in the position they were all in today. He knew it was either Wendell or himself, or both. The chief's eyes were still on him as he waited for some kind of response.

"He have it, I swear. I did hide it in the ceiling and he is the only person I tell. When I come back home the ceiling was open. He trying to set me up for the money."

The chief turned back to Wendell and then took a step back. He looked at the officer who brought him in.

"He don't have anything on him sir. We check the

car, it not there either," the officer said.

"Check the bedroom," the chief said and they'd both allowed Wendell's almost lifeless body to fall to the ground and went into the bedroom. The chief took that time to finish drinking his water.

Fifteen minutes after they came out of the bedroom showing the gun to the chief. He asked how much rounds were in the magazine and was satisfied with their answer. They left the gun at the counter and waited for further instructions.

"Listen." The chief was talking to both Wendell and Kevin. "I have plenty things to do with my life, if allyuh don't value allyuh life that is not my problem. I want that memory card, and I want it now. If I don't get it I going to start killing from ah side. So allyuh have a decision to make."

Wendell was watching the chief with his eyes almost shut. He was breathing very slowly.

The chief was thinking for a while and then pointed to Wendell. He was ready to prove his point. Both officers held him to his feet once more. The chief went to him with the gun in his hand and made sure there was a round in the chamber.

"I going to ask allyuh one more time. Where the memory card?" Wendell looked in the chief's eyes and then looked at Kevin.

Kevin bent his head in shame. He heard Wendell cursed loudly and within the second that he brought his eyes back at them he saw Wendell spit a mouthful of blood into the chief's face.

Kevin felt like everything was happening in slow

motion. The look in Wendell's eyes as he knew he was going to die and the officers as they moved towards their chief who hadn't even budged. Both officers were still holding up his hands and they turned away when the chief lifted the gun to Wendell's face.

He pulled the trigger and brought time back to its normal speed. Blood splattered on the wall and both officers allowed Wendell's body to fall to the ground.

The chief pulled out a rag and wiped his face. He then threw the gun next to Wendell's body and started walking towards the door.

"What you want we to do with him?" the talker was asking about Kevin.

"Do what you does do best. And make sure this house is flattened."

"Roger..."

The chief had given them the instruction to kill Kevin and burn the evidence.

Kevin was willing to try anything now. His hands felt numb and his heart was trying its best to escape his chest. His stomach felt so tight that he was only allowed to inhale and exhale through his mouth.

He looked at Wendell's body and reminded himself that everything that had just happened was real, and wherever Wendell had gone he would be there soon if he didn't try something, anything at all.

"Sir..." he called out to the chief while he was already out of the door. He stopped and turned around. His face was clean. There were only traces of blood on his suit.

"What?" he said, annoyed.

"I think I know where he hide the memory card."

The chief looked at him, trying to read him. He shook his head. "After all this, you now want to talk. Give me one good reason why I should even listen to you."

Kevin started thinking. He knew he wanted to live and he would do anything, but that might not be the best answer. He also wanted to get back his life, which wasn't yet discussed and there was no telling what could happen after he handed over the memory card to them. So, he eliminated that answer too.

He thought about his girlfriend and his unborn child. They meant more than the world to him, and he was one hundred percent sure that they'd never betray him.

"Because I going to be a first-time father and I know if I go against my word you have the power to take that away from me and I don't want that." He looked at the chief. The chief was listening.

"So, that is why I wouldn't lie to you. Plus, that is the only place we ever hide anything. It is an abandoned house in the bush. I would take you there and if it not there you could kill me."

"Hmm." The chief smiled. "You know, I like how that sounding. I just hope you don't do like yuh friend and try to spit in my face."

Kevin shook his head. "Sir, with all due respect, my mother raised me better than that."

He nodded. "And I would like to meet yuh mother someday. Maybe if things doesn't go the way we plan, I could arrange ah family reunion." He gave it some thought and then smiled and gestured for his officers to untie him."

"What about the place?" the officer asked.

"That one still stand. It too risky. Burn everything. I

would write on it." He turned and walked away.

Two officers left and went outside, and another went into the kitchen and turned on the gas while the one who was doing all the talking untied Kevin.

Kevin felt the blood rush back into his hands and his chest expanded as he took in large gulps of air.

When he was completely untied the two officers returned with two bottles of gas.

Kevin stood up and the officer held his hand and reached for his handcuffs.

The door was wide open, and Kevin saw a possibility of freedom. He had done it before and gotten away. If not now he'd have to escape eventually since there wouldn't be any memory card to be found once the house was destroyed. He'd have to think fast and make a run for it before the handcuffs went on.

He looked around at the other officers and noted where their guns were.

The officer in the kitchen was still standing guard but the two others were using both hands to pour the gas throughout the rooms.

Wendell's body was already covered with gas.

Kevin looked outside. There was a space between the vehicles where he could pass, and the vehicles would take most of the shots.

He kept his eyes on two officers who were smoking in a corner outside next to the vehicles.

One hand was snapped with the handcuff and the officer reached for the other hand. Kevin knew that it was either now or never.

He pulled his hand away and dealt the officer a blow

to the face, causing him to fall to ground and he made a run for the door. He heard the officer in the kitchen shout out to the others and that was when he heard several loud explosions coming from behind him. He felt a burn on his foot and then another on his back. He gasped for air, and then felt another burn on his lower back and his body slumped to the ground like a puppet with cut strings.

CHAPTER FOURTEEN

As Kevin opened his eyes he tried to battle the sunlight that was shining onto his face through the large window that was almost the size of the wall. He turned to the opposite side and saw a police officer sitting on a chair near his bed, reading a newspaper. He had a weathered face and close-cropped hair that was almost entirely white.

"Morning," the officer said when he noticed that Kevin had awakened. Kevin didn't answer, but attempted to sit up. Only then did he realize that a pair of handcuffs chained his left hand and his right ankle to the bed. He lay back down. "Morning officer," he said.

"I almost thought you forget yuh manners," said the policeman.

"No, is not that," Kevin replied. His chest and throat pained a little as he talked.

"Somebody wake up on the wrong side of the bed?"

Kevin didn't answer, he just turned and continued looking around the room.

The room was a lot smaller than most of the hospital rooms he had seen, and his bed was the only bed in the room. There were a few medical charts on the wall, outlining proper hygienic practices. The door was behind the officer and Kevin could see doctors and nurses on the other side of it.

The room smelled far better than the room that Steve had been in. Kevin thought that it was probably because of the fact that the room was only designed to hold one patient.

He hated the idea of being hospitalized under those circumstances, but he was grateful for the care and the fact that he was still alive.

His throat felt dry.

"What time breakfast coming?" he asked.

The officer looked at the time on his watch.

"Is almost eight. Normally it does be here around eight, eight-thirty for the latest."

"Okay…"

"If you really that hungry I don't mind organizing it for you now."

Kevin shook his head.

"Nah, I will hold on. I could do with some water though."

"Uh… okay." The officer shifted on the chair and Kevin saw three bottles of water on the table next to him. One was almost empty. There were also a few snacks and some fruits. The officer checked the temperature of the two full bottles.

"You could have one of mines. I eh open it yet, but it not that cold."

"Yeah, no problem." The officer opened it and handed it to him.

Kevin sat up and drank all of it before handing the empty bottle back to the officer who threw it into a bin at the side of the door without getting up from his chair.

"Good aim," Kevin said.

The policeman grinned and started reading his newspaper again.

Kevin was thinking. He had no idea what his medical condition was or what had happened to his apartment. Had it been burned down or not? And what would be his situation when the hospital was finished with him?

"So, officer...?" Kevin said.

"Gibson… Corporal Gibson," the officer said and folded the newspaper.

"How I end up here?"

The corporal face looked confused. "What you mean by that?"

"I mean, how I reach here? Police bring me in?" Kevin asked, wondering why they'd bring him in when all their worries would've come to an end if they'd killed him. He was trying to figure out if they had something else planned for him.

"Oh. No. The ambulance bring you in. Some of yuh neighbours hear the shooting and when they went to see what was taking place, they saw you lying there. Somebody called for the ambulance and it was right in the area. You lucky, because they usual take a while. If that was the case. I don't think you woulda make it."

"Oh, so the officers wasn't the ones who called the ambulance?"

"Well yeah. I believe so. That is the normal protocol. But one of yuh neighbours did also call to find out how far they was."

Kevin was quiet. He realized that his neighbours were actually the ones who had saved his life. If it wasn't for them there was a great possibility that the officers would've stalled and left him there to die. He was glad that his neighbours had intervened.

He thought in silence for a while.

He said, "I know you might not be able to give out certain information, but I just want to find out something else."

"Yeah, no problem, go ahead."

"Well, I can't remember everything that happen. All I remember was being in my house with them officers and then waking up here," Kevin said, hoping that he had said enough to lead the conversation. The corporal was waiting for him to finish what he had to say. But Kevin said nothing.

"Okay," the corporal said, finally. "So you remember being there with yuh friend Wendell?"

"Ye-ah…" Kevin answered, knowing very well that his answer couldn't go without the explanation.

"And the officers breaking down yuh door to respond to the shooting?"

Kevin became confused.

"No." He shook his head. "The officers didn't break down the door."

"So, you don't remember that part either?"

"Well, I remember the officers being there, but they didn't break down the door to come inside."

"So, how they get inside then?"

"They pick the lock."

The corporal glanced at him from the corner of his eyes as if he thought Kevin was being ridiculous. He waited a few seconds, giving Kevin the opportunity to correct himself, but when he realized Kevin wasn't saying anything he continued talking.

"So, what you telling me is that the officers responded to a shooting at your house, and took their time to pick the lock to get inside the house?"

"Um..." Kevin realized how stupid it was sounding. He knew he'd have to go in-depth with the story if he wanted the corporal to understand the situation, but that wasn't something he was prepared to do since he didn't know if the corporal was part of their crew.

"Okay, this is what happened. I went to my house to get some money and clothes and other stuff and before I could leave the officers picked the lock to come inside and lock me up."

"Okay." The corporal nodded. "And how yuh friend Wendell come into the picture?"

Kevin only wanted the corporal to reveal whether his apartment was burnt down or not, so he'd know whether the memory card was still in play. But the situation was turning out more complicated than he had expected.

"He was my driver. He dropped me there to collect my stuff and he came back to pick me up when I called him."

"Okay, and the officers follow him there and pick the lock to get inside?"

"Yeah."

The corporal leaned back on the chair and crossed his feet as if he was a shrink, studying the complicated mind of his patient. He looked very calm while doing so.

"So, what about Wendell family?"

Kevin raised his brow when he heard the corporal mention the family. He had almost forgotten about them.

"Hmm." He sighed. "What about them?"

He waited a few seconds before answering. "They went to the station and made a report that you assaulted his sister before tying them up and going to meet Wendell."

Kevin nervously passed his hand through his hair and on his face. He kept his fist over his mouth. "That was all they say?"

"From the information I get, yeah." They were both silent for a short moment. "So it is true?"

"Well…" Kevin was contemplating whether to tell the truth or not and decided that lying would only make things more complicated. "Yeah, somewhat." He shook his head, disappointed in himself for what he had done.

"So, what exactly is true? Everything or just the report his family make?"

Kevin looked at him as if he was crazy to be asking such a question.

"Only what his family say. Wendell was my friend. We had we ups and downs in the past, but I would never think about doing something like that."

"Okay, calm down. I not here to interrogate you or anything. We just talking, right?"

"Yeah. I know… I normal."

The corporal was thinking.

"So, if you don't mind me asking, what was yuh

intentions after tying up his family?"

Kevin looked at him and shook his head. He was beginning to sound more and more like an investigator and Kevin was becoming annoyed.

"Listen, this whole thing plenty bigger than you think okay. And no matter what I say, it not going to make a difference. So we could just forget about it for now, alright?"

The corporal frowned.

"Alright, I understand what you saying but let me just explain something," he said. "I just here to guard you, nothing else. Now that you wake up, I have to call the investigator who dealing with this matter and he would send his people to stay with you until you medically fit to stand trial. I not even supposed to be talking to you. And, because of that, I can't mention any of this. So, don't worry." He was studying Kevin's reaction. "So, now that, that out of the way," he continued. "Hear what. You tell me exactly what you want to know and I would tell you just that. This whole situation too confusing for me to deal with anyways."

Kevin thought about all the things he would want to know.

"Okay, well... What is the information you get concerning Wendell?"

"Well, based on the investigation, they working with the theory that he wanted to turn you in for the reward money so you killed him," the corporal said.

Kevin slapped his hand on the bed, then looked up at the ceiling in disbelief. He then took a deep breath and tightened his fist, in an attempt to control his anger. It was like the police were working overtime to make sure he'd have to spend the rest of his life behind bars, since they didn't succeed in killing him. It was beginning to seem impossible to get out of their mess.

He looked at the corporal.

"And what about my apartment?"

"Well, you didn't succeed in burning the evidence. You end up pouring the gas, but the officers came in time to stop you in yuh tracks."

"By shooting me?"

The corporal shook his head. "What else you expect? You shoot behind the police and run out…"

"I didn't shoot behind no fucking police," Kevin said, angrily, then stopped. He took in a deep breath and exhaled slowly. "Sorry, is not even your fault." He shook his head and turned to the window. The corporal gave him a few minutes to calm himself.

"Anything else?" he asked.

Before Kevin could reply, an attendant entered the room. She was pushing a trolley that contained boxes of food and drinks. She seemed surprised that Kevin was awake.

"Morning. I didn't know the patient was up," she said to the corporal as she handed him his breakfast and a cup of tea. He took it and rested it on top of the table right next to the newspapers.

"Yeah, he wake up a short while ago."

"I would tell the nurses and when they finish with him I will come back with his breakfast, okay?"

"Alright, no problem."

The corporal stood up and went to the door. The

nurse was smiling with him.

"Don't forget to let me know when you leaving," she said to him.

"Yeah, don't worry. I would check you as soon as they reach."

"Alright, I hope so," she said blushing, and left the room. He had a broad smile that took a while to go away.

He returned to his seat and asked Kevin if there was anything else he wanted to know for the second time, and when Kevin shook his head the corporal got up and contacted someone on his cell phone, telling them that the patient had awoken.

Two Nigerian doctors came into the room a short while after and during their conversation with the corporal Kevin learnt that he was shot four times. Twice in his back, and twice in his left leg. Luckily for him there wasn't any major damage done to his organs and there was also a drastic improvement with the internal bleeding. The corporal took notes.

After the doctors left, the smiling attendant returned with Kevin's breakfast, which was a bread and tuna sandwich and a lukewarm cup of tea. Before he had finished eating several officers came into the room and were greeted by the corporal. They were all dressed in the blue and black tactical wear and equipped with machine guns, and unlike the officers at Kevin's apartment, their faces were not hidden.

One of the men told the corporal that they were the officers who were specifically assigned to continue the guard duty until the patient was discharged. He also mentioned that each officer was assigned to work a twelve-hour rotation period.

After their discussion the corporal left without saying a word to Kevin, but he made eye contact and that was when Kevin remembered that he said he wasn't supposed to say anything to him.

The officers were briefed and then taken outside to be introduced to the doctors and nurses who were assigned to Kevin. When that was completed, the officers came back in the room.

They walked around and looked under the bed and mattress for anything out of the ordinary. When they were satisfied only one of the officers remained. He secured the windows and went outside the door. He checked on Kevin once or twice within every hour.

The first few nights passed uneasily, as Kevin had to learn to sleep with limited movements due to his hand and foot being cuffed to the bed. He also had pains from the bullet wounds and other bruises.

The doctors and nurses had their specific visiting times, so during the night when his pain became unbearable they would only attend to him on their timing. On a few occasions the officer on duty would come to him and quiet him down by making threats to harm him since he was also interrupting their sleep. All that had stopped when Kevin had learned that the pain he was feeling was nothing compared to what they did to him when he didn't keep his mouth shut.

Tuesday morning after breakfast a slim East Indian man entered the room. He was dressed in a suit and carrying a folder under his arm. His head was bald, and his face was clean shaven. Kevin thought that he was either in his late forties or early fifties. He walked straight to the bed and sat on the chair where the corporal was once seated without looking Kevin directly in the face. He made himself comfortable before saying anything.

"Morning, how everything going with you?" he said and waited for Kevin's response.

"I good for the hour," Kevin answered, wondering who he was.

"Alright, good." He looked relaxed and unbothered. "My name is Jason Ramoutar. I attached to the Arima CID, and I is the main investigator in your case."

Kevin gave him his attention.

He opened the folder and began studying the first page as if it was the first time he was looking at it.

"Kevin Jones, age twenty eight of 54 Kenneth Street, Enterprise," he said with a half-smile and then closed the file and kept his eyes on Kevin for a moment.

"You know, for the past few weeks I was working hard on this case, and I was trying to figure out how somebody like you end up in all this mess. I mean. I was dying to know where you went wrong. You don't have any criminal record and you never had any problems with the law before. But, after digging deeper I realize after getting lay off from your work early last year you started hanging out with Steve Thomas, Marcus Elliot and Wendell Pierre. All three of them had drug related offenses before the court. I think hanging with them fellas was the first bad decision you make. And I believe that is the problem."

Kevin was looking at him and listening. He was impressed by what he had gathered from the investigation and was anxious to know what else he knew.

"I have my theory of what went on at that nightclub and things not looking too good on your part."

"And what is your theory?" Kevin said.

He smiled. "I glad you ask. That mean you willing to cooperate." He opened back the file and turned the page.

Kevin remained quiet.

"Okay, this is the facts I have. You and yuh boys have allyuh little drug thing going on. So somebody arrange a birthday lime for the deceased, Marcus Elliot and everybody attended, all good and well. Except, you had something else up your sleeve. Yuh girlfriend pregnant and like any father you want the best for your child, so you decide to get rid of everyone in the crew and take everything for yourself and head south for the winter." He paused and looked at Kevin with a smirk on his face and then shook his head as if he was disappointed in him.

Kevin bit down on his jaw and looked away for a moment. He was eager to intervene, but he'd decided to listen to everything the investigator had to say, before speaking.

"After killing Marcus and leaving Steve in his critical condition you went into the Brasso Seco forest with the intentions to lay low for a few days." He turned the page again and scan through before he continued with his story.

"Unfortunately for you, our officers went into quick action and they eventually caught up with you in the forest. You fired at the officers and somehow managed to escape." He looked up at Kevin to make sure he was following.

"After hiding for a few days you contact Wendell and

convince him that you didn't have anything to do with the shooting at the club. He believed you, as expected, and the both of you arranged to meet at your house for whatever reason. At that time a reward was already on your head and Wendell decide to go against allyuh friendship and turn you in for the money. You found out his plan and put a bullet to his head without showing any remorse. The gunshot alerted the police and within no time police broke down your door and you started shooting behind them yet again. But, this time you wasn't so lucky, hence the reason why you lying on this hospital bed here today." He closed the file and was smiling.

Kevin shook his head and turned away. He could feel the anger and frustration building inside him. They had done everything necessary to clear their tracks.

"So, what you think?" the investigator finally said.

Kevin turned to him and used his free hand to wipe away the tears from his eyes.

"What you mean what I think? You know that is not what happen."

"Well, let me share ah little something with you. Is not always about what happen. A lot of times it is about what you could prove happen. And, unlike you, we could prove all of this."

Kevin thought about it and he knew, even with the memory card he couldn't prove much. The evidence on the memory card wouldn't be enough to prove he was innocent in the nightclub's shooting, or in Wendell's murder.

"So, what you want?"

The investigator showed a straight face now. "Nothing

much, but before we get into that let me just say something. You see how important it is to not interfere. It is always better to mind your own business. If you did just leave that memory card where it was, none of this would be happening today." He leaned closer to Kevin and lowered his voice. "Too much people involve in this operation. So, I hope you understand why we couldn't just leave it like that."

"Hmm…" Kevin was thinking. "So allyuh not going to back down until allyuh get that memory card?" he said in a weakened voice.

"No. And that is one of the reason you alive today. We didn't want to take the chance of it getting in the wrong hands."

"Yeah, that obvious. I figured that much. And what I getting in exchange for the memory card?"

He opened the folder to a page where Kevin could see a few loose pages.

"It real simple. All you have to do is cooperate. We would send a lawyer for you and all you have to do is sign a confession statement."

Kevin heart raced on the thought of getting a sentence of life imprisonment for committing both murders. His eyes where opened wide. "A confession statement of what? Your theory?"

"No, of course not. We have another conclusion. It going to benefit you more because you would be serving less jail time."

"How much less?"

"Anywhere between five to eight years."

Kevin thought about it. He knew they had already

done a good job in tarnishing his name. At this point he knew they were capable of doing anything in order to stay out of prison.

"And what about Steve?"

The investigator looked surprised by the question.

"What about him?"

"He getting charge for anything?"

"No. Unless you want to give us some information, we don't have anything on him. We have a good idea that he still dealing with drugs. But, that is all we have. We don't have any concrete evidence."

Kevin was glad to hear that.

"So, let me get this straight. The deal is, I would be getting less jail time and you guys would continue doing what allyuh doing without the fear of eventually getting caught by whoever would have access to the memory card?"

"Yeah, exactly. Is a win-win situation for everybody. Unless you decide to serve the life sentence. That way it would only be a win situation for us." He smiled a crooked officer kind of smile.

Kevin was given an ultimatum, but serving anything less than a life sentence would be the obvious decision.

"What is the new story?" he asked.

The investigator shifted the loose pages. "Well, we willing to take you off of the nightclub shooting by pinning everything on Wendell. We would even make it clear that he went to your house to finish what he started at the club and you somehow managed to call the police. When we reach there, you ran through the door and he shot you a couple times. At that moment, we had no choice but to take him down."

"Okay, and what about my face being all over the news?"

"That is what you can't get away from and we had no choice but to add it in your statement." His eyes went back to the folder. "So, after the nightclub shooting you were fearful for your life and went hiding in the forest, hoping that things would clear up and we would find Wendell before he find you. While searching the forest for suspects we caught up with you and you managed to shoot yuh way out. Luckily no officers did get hurt." He handed both statements to Kevin so he could examine them.

Both documents were a combination of the investigator's summary of the evidence he had gathered and Kevin's confession statement.

The new statement cleared him of both murders along with some other major offences. It was a good deal.

Kevin's eyes left the pages and went to the investigator.

"What? Something wrong?" He asked when he noticed Kevin's concerned look.

"How I so sure you would keep your end of the deal?"

He smiled. "That is the best part. You would only give us the memory card after yuh first hearing. As long as the judge see the statement you good to go. It don't have anything we could say or do to change that."

"Oh, okay." Kevin continued studying both statements for some time.

"So, we have a deal?" the investigator interrupted his reading.

"Yeah. We have ah deal." Kevin said without taking his eyes off of the documents.

"Okay, good."

The investigator stood up and walked over to the window where he contacted the lawyer and gave him the okay to come in.

When Kevin had finished reading the statements he returned it to the investigator who then left the room.

The lawyer came during the afternoon of the following day. The officer left the door opened and stood outside the room, giving them their privacy.

The lawyer greeted him and immediately went into his briefcase, taking out the necessary documents. He kept it in his hand and looked to the door, scanning the area.

"Mister Ramoutar explained everything to you already?" he asked.

"Yeah."

"Okay, and you understand everything he told you?"

"Yeah, I want to believe so."

The lawyer was staring at him as if he was looking forward to a question, but after waiting a few seconds he handed over the document and a pen.

"This very straightforward. All I need you to do is read it through and once you don't have any problem, you would put your signature here." He pointed to the line where Kevin was required to sign at the bottom of the last page and he took a seat.

Kevin took some time to read all four pages, and when he was finished he acknowledged that it was the same as the previous one. The lawyer noticed that he had stopped reading and stood up.

"You finish?"

"Yeah."

"Okay." There wasn't any signature and he waited a while before asking if there was a problem.

"No, but I just want to find out what is the procedure from here."

"Okay." He straightened up. "Well, once you sign it I would communicate with Mister Ramoutar and we would start working out the charges."

Kevin became concerned about the amount of charges he would be facing.

"How much charges I looking at?"

"Well." He looked to the door again and then leaned closer to Kevin to keep the conversation between them. "I going to work it out in order for you to get the least amount of charges from these offences. But don't worry, me and Ramoutar working together to make sure you don't get anything more than eight years. That was the deal and we sticking to that."

Kevin felt relieved, and he nodded his appreciation. The lawyer seemed happy too.

"Okay. So as soon as you sign this I would be able to go back to my office and start cutting down these charges."

Kevin scratched his signature on the line and gave the pen and the document back to him. He examined it carefully before putting it into his briefcase. He was ready to leave.

"Okay, so let me go back and start working on this. Once I finish before you get discharge you would see me here. If not, I would see you at the station to confirm everything and you would put your final signatures, okay?"

"Yeah, cool."

He walked out the room and the door closed behind him.

As time passed Kevin realized that he was in hospital and he was already feeling more confined than a prisoner. His only hope was that Shantel wouldn't be ashamed of him and she would bring his child to visit him occasionally while in prison.

Some nights he found himself crying as it was difficult to deal with the feeling of being all alone and hopeless. He was surrounded by four dark walls with no TV, music, or connection to the outside world. The only comfort he had during the late hours of the night were the voices in his head, telling him that he would soon be out of the hospital and off to a prison where there would at least be some sought of interaction with reality and visiting hours.

On the fourth week he was removed from a number of machines and the major tubes were also taken out. The doctors had come to him and informed him that, once everything went well, he would be discharged in two weeks time.

It was the best news he had gotten since the morning he woke up at hospital and it was also the first time he had smiled since he was there.

Motivated by the news he had spent the remaining time exercising his body by doing some, simple awkward crunches on the bed along with stretches and other short movements.

During his final week the officers had uncuffed him from the bed and kept only his legs chained. He was allowed to move around the room and he took full advantage of the situation by pushing his body to the limit. He would do everything from push-ups, sit-ups, crunches and jumps.

On the morning that he was carded to be discharged, he'd woken up before sunrise and did his usual early morning workout and then went standing at the window, awaiting the sunrise. It was the first time he'd done that.

He felt like a new man and he knew he looked like one to.

He had a beard now, and although he was slim he could see and feel his rock-hard abs, hands and legs.

He was disappointed that he had lost the battle against the officers, but he had won something much more important and that was the ability to survive whatever they threw at him.

He closed his eyes and allowed the sun to consume his body. He then stretched out his hands like an eagle would spread its wings. It was exactly what he needed to rejuvenate.

At that moment it was clear to him that he was the only person in control of his future. And, win, lose or draw he'd have to remain in control.

The door opened and he felt someone enter the room. He didn't move, just listened carefully.

"Aye, muscle head."

It was one of the officers and he knew exactly who it was without opening his eyes or dropping his hands. He shook his head to the petty remark.

"Start organizing. We leaving in an hour's time."

Kevin remained quiet. He opened his eyes and

enjoyed the view.

When he heard the door close he turned and went to the bathroom to do as the officer instructed.

After the doctor and nurses were gone, four officers entered the room. They handcuffed him and escorted Kevin out of the hospital and into an awaiting police vehicle downstairs.

He was dressed in a hospital gown and was given the opportunity to contact someone of his choice when he arrived at the Central Police station, to bring a change of clothes for him to attend court the following morning.

Kevin admired his surroundings. Although it was everything he was used to, he enjoyed being in the midst of it once again.

There were three police vehicles and as they exited the hospital's compound they made their way through the streets with the sirens screaming at pedestrians and vehicles to get out of their way.

Kevin was in the vehicle in the middle and his body was being thrown from side to side as the vehicle swerved around other vehicles and took some sharp corners.

Traffic lights meant nothing to them as they burst their way through, getting full respect from oncoming vehicles.

It took them a little less than ten minutes before they came to a sudden stop in front of the police station.

To Kevin's surprise he could see a crowd of pedestrians waiting to see what was taking place. He could already feel the embarrassment as the reporters waited to the front to get a clear shot at him for nothing more than a headline story.

Two officers opened the back and helped Kevin out.

The flashes started immediately, and voices could be heard from the crowd as they all tried to voice their opinion at the same time.

Kevin kept his head turned away from the commotion as he was being hurried to the station's entrance, protected by a barricade of four additional officers.

It seemed as though there were reporters everywhere as the police were being prompted to answer questions as they made their way up the steps. They hadn't said anything.

On the inside Kevin was presented to an officer who was sitting behind a desk. He was dressed in casual clothing and was seen delegating officers to carry out certain functions. After writing Kevin's information in a log book the officer instructed them to start processing him and then take him to a cell which they had prepared for him in the back.

They led him into a room where they took his finger prints and filled out the necessary forms. He was then allowed one phone call. He thought about reliability and contacted his cousin who lived in Port-of-Spain. He requested a suit and a change of clothes and his cousin said that he would be there after work.

Kevin was led through the halls and placed into the first empty cell. As his hands and feet were being freed from the cuffs he could hear shouts coming from the other cells as prisoners called for food and drinks while some pleaded for a hearing as they swore their innocence.

It was Kevin's first time in a prison cell. He had only heard stories of the poor conditions.

Inside the cell was dark, since the overhead lights weren't working. The first thing that caused some discomfort was the scent of sweat and faeces that filled the air. There was a small vent about twelve feet up but that wasn't enough to filter the air, much less rid the room of its odour.

There was a metal toilet bowl and basin on one side of the room and a concrete bench to the right of it where discoloured newspapers were spread across like it had been used by everyone who came in.

The cell was not designed to cater for privacy or comfort.

Kevin felt his stomach turn and he began to feel lightheaded. Within a short moment sweat had already covered his skin and he was in desperate need of water and something to eat.

He stood close to the iron bars where he would catch the first set of almost-fresh air that came down the hallway.

The voices of the prisoners next to him would often distract him from his situation.

As more time passed his thirst was becoming unbearable. The water in the tap looked contaminated by the rusty pipelines but he felt as though he had no other choice. He drank from the pipe and returned to the iron bars where he sat on the ground and waited.

A few hours passed, and two officers came with a box containing lunches. After distributing it they took some time to explain to the rowdy prisoner that whatever problems he had, he'd have to take it up with the magistrate the following morning. After mentioning that several times to the same individual, Kevin saw them walking away annoyed by the prisoner's lack of understanding. They told Kevin that his lawyer was on the way.

Outside was already dark when the lawyer arrived. The officers had taken them into a room where the lawyer sat opposite Kevin at a wooden desk.

There weren't any windows in the room just the desk, two cameras and an air conditioning unit. Both officers stood at the door.

"How everything going with you?" the lawyer said, while taking out the documents from inside his briefcase. Kevin wasn't sure if he should answer the question. He knew that speaking the truth would cause some tension and he was already enjoying being out of the cell for the few minutes.

"Well, all I could say is thank God for life," Kevin said.

The lawyer smiled, though the true answer seemed obvious to him.

He placed his briefcase on the ground, leaving only the documents and a pen on the table. He started flipping through the pages.

"Well I worked out everything and I got a total of fourteen charges." He paused and looked at Kevin who was looking right back at him. Kevin was wondering what it meant in terms of jail sentencing.

"That is about seven and a half years in prison, could be less, knowing you don't have any previous conviction. But, at the end of the day. That is all up to the judge."

Kevin was quiet. For him there wasn't anything to be happy about. After seeing the condition of the cell, all he could think about was framing his mind to spend seven years in similar conditions.

The lawyer seemed unsatisfied for some reason. "Just remember this could've been a lot worst," he continued. "I bypassed a lot of minor offences in order to keep it below eight years… okay?"

"Yeah," Kevin finally said. "I not upset or anything. You do what you say you was going to do. So… thanks."

"Yeah, sure. No problem. I just doing my job." He turned the document and guided it over to Kevin.

"Just read it through and if you need me to clear up anything, just ask, okay? If not, I would just need you to sign on the last page so I could take it for the inspector to sign." Kevin lifted the pen and began turning the page.

"Take your time."

Kevin browsed through the pages. There were fourteen pages and each page were labeled notice to prisoner. Kevin read charges from escaping lawful custody, procession of an illegal firearm, malicious damage, damage to government property, and more. On the last page he noticed that he was to be charged for shooting with intent to cause grievous bodily harm. He turned the page again and his eyes focused on the dotted lines. He looked to the door and he could see the officer on the opposite side looking right back at him. He then took up the pen and hesitated for a while as he thought about the possibility of being tricked. Nevertheless, he scribbled his signature, hoping that everything would work out the way they'd explained.

The lawyer carefully compared his signature with another document and then placed the pages back into his briefcase. He signaled the officers, then got up and thanked Kevin and the officers for their time and left the room.

Kevin was taken back to his cell.

CHAPTER FIFTEEN

Kevin had almost drifted away in sleep when he lifted his head, distracted by a tapping sound on the bar. He saw a man holding up a suit in one hand and a bag in the other. He couldn't see the person clearly from where he was lying on the bench.

He got up and as he walked closer he noticed that it was a police officer dressed in the grey and blue uniform with stripes on his sleeve. It was the first officer he saw attending to prisoners in that uniform since he was brought in.

Kevin reached up to the bars and he smiled when he noticed who it was.

The corporal smiled back at him.

"What you doing here?" Kevin said in a most grateful voice.

"I work here, remember?"

Kevin was glad to see someone he knew.

He studied the suit that the corporal was holding in his hand. It was a black suit with a white shirt. It was neatly pressed and kept in one of those clear suit bags. Kevin could tell that the other clothes he'd asked for was in the black plastic bag in his other hand.

Corporal Gibson passed it through the bars and Kevin took it and rested it on the bench and returned to him.

"So, what? You working tonight or something?"

"Yeah, I come on for eight."

"Okay, cool."

"Yeah, I finishing in the morning. How everything was with you today?"

Kevin quickly recapped the day.

"Well, this is a first-time experience for me, so I just getting used to it. I can't complain. Lunch and dinner was ah little late, but at least I eat, right?"

"True."

Corporal Gibson seemed to have something on his mind. "How everything with you though?" Kevin asked, hoping that his question would give the corporal some sort of encouragement to open up.

"Well. I holding it down for now. I in charge of this shift so I have some paper work and some other things to finish up. But, other than that. Everything just normal."

"Okay."

The place was quiet for a while and the corporal walked to the other cells and observed the prisoners for a moment before returning. His concern was more obvious now.

Kevin's anxiety was building and he couldn't hold in the anticipation any longer. "You sure you good? You looking like you have something on yuh mind."

He studied Kevin for a moment. "Well, I was watching through the files and I see you decide to confess?"

"Oh, yeah." Kevin reminded himself that the corporal was the person in charge and it was obvious that he would have access to all the files concerning the prisoners.

"I think everything will work out better this way."

"Well, true. But, that is not what bothering me though." The corporal looked concerned. Kevin held onto the bars and leaned closer to him. He was very interested to hear what the corporal was about to say.

"I trying to understand why you thought you had to lie about it in the first place?"

Kevin released the bars and took a step back, trying to come to terms with what the corporal was saying.

"What you talking about? I didn't lie."

"I talking about Wendell. I ask if you was the one who killed him and you did say no."

"Yeah, and that was the truth. I didn't lie. I tell you before, that me and Wendell was good friends and…"

"Okay, yeah, I know." He lifted his hand, cutting Kevin across. "I remember what you tell me. But, if that is the case, why you confess to killing him if you know you didn't do it?"

"I didn't confess to. Wait… what?" Kevin couldn't believe what he had just heard. He could feel the tension rising as he walked back to the bars. "What you mean, I confess to the killing? I didn't confess to killing anybody."

Corporal Gibson shook his head and smiled and started walking away. Kevin could tell that his smile was meant to be a disguise for his frustration. He stopped a few feet away and turned back to the cell.

"Who you think I is? You take me for ah fool or something?"

"What? No… I would never do that. You suppose to know me better than that." Kevin walked closer to where the corporal was standing. "Listen, I confess to certain things but I didn't kill anybody so I didn't confess to killing nobody. I telling you the truth. Why you not believing me?"

"Hmm." Corporal Gibson sighed. "Why? Why I should even believe you when you telling me one thing and telling them a whole different story?"

Kevin thought about his question. It lingered in his mind as he relived the signing process, trying to remember where he'd gone wrong. He couldn't recall anything suspicious. On both occasions he had read the documents word by word before putting his signature. The only thing he could've thought of was the possibility of them forging his signature.

"That is what I thought," said Corporal Gibson, as Kevin failed to answer his question. He turned to walk away.

"No wait," Kevin said, stopping him. "I was just trying to remember what went on."

"Hmm." The corporal shook his head. Their eyes were locked on each other. "So now you trying to tell me you can't remember making that confession?"

"No." Kevin lifted his hand and started shaking his head as if he was having a nervous breakdown. "I remember making a confession, but not on anything concerning ah murder."

The corporal turned away and took a short breath

and exhaled long and hard. He started thinking. Kevin observed him quietly.

After a few minutes he shook his head in disappointment. “Listen, I trying to talk to you but if you plan to continue like this, having this conversation wouldn’t make any sense,” he said and folded his arms across his chest. Within a short time Kevin was beginning to feel intimidated by the way the corporal was just standing there watching him.

“Okay, on the document you see. How much charges you saw me confess to?” Kevin asked, breaking the silence.

The corporal waited a few seconds before answering. “About forty something, why?”

“Because, the confession I make was only fourteen charges. I remember flipping through the fourteen pages and then signing at the back of the last one. All the information was on one side of the page and the opposite side was blank. Except for the last page.” He could tell that the corporal wasn’t understanding where he was getting at.

“I know this whole thing sounding confusing, but I could prove that I telling the truth. I remember seeing ah camera in the room. If you look back at the cameras, you would see that I only flipped through fourteen pages, not forty like what you saying.”

The corporal looked as though he was considering it. He was studying something for a short moment before speaking.

“So, you saying it only had fourteen charges in your confession?” he asked in a low concerned voice.

“Yeah, and it didn’t have nothing about any murder.”

"Hmm, okay." The corporal started walking away. "I have some things to organize, but I would check it once I get a chance."

Kevin blew out a breath of relief. He then stuck his hands through the bars with his palms together. "Thanks. I would really appreciate if you check it, because you would see for yourself and realize that I telling you the truth."

The corporal turned and quietly walked away. Kevin waited a while and then went to the bench and took a seat. There were a lot of thoughts going through his mind and that made it very difficult for him to focus on one thing for more than a few seconds. He was uneasy as he anxiously waited for the corporal to return from reviewing the cameras.

About an hour after he heard someone approaching and as he hoped for the best he finally saw the corporal appear at his cell. He looked worried. Kevin got up and went to him.

"You get a chance to look at the cameras?" Kevin spoke first.

"Yeah." The corporal looked at him and nodded with a frown. It seemed as though his mind was somewhere else.

"And?"

"Well, yeah… It really had fourteen pages.

Kevin smiled and slapped his hand on the bar, expressing his relief. "See what I tell you? I don't have any reason to lie for something like that. Especially to you."

"Yeah." The corporal was quiet for a moment. "Something here not adding up?" he finally said to himself.

Kevin waited a while and noticed that the corporal was in deep thoughts and was mumbling something to himself every now and then.

"You alright?" Kevin said.

"Yeah, I good." He straightened up and looked at Kevin. "You have any idea why they would want to put all them extra charges on you?"

Kevin shifted to the side and leaned his back against the wall. He was putting some thought into the situation. He understood what the corporal was asking and as much as he didn't want to go into depths when they were back at the hospital, he knew that this was what it had come down to. He remembered the night it had all started and the incident that had led him to the drug house. He looked at the corporal who was hoping for an answer that would bring some sought of understanding to the situation.

"Ah little while ago when you come back from watching the tape, I hear you say, something wasn't adding up. What make you say that?" Kevin said in a low voice, trying to analyze whether he was a worthy enough person to confide in. Kevin said this without looking in his direction.

"Because I working in this service long enough to know, police not going to throw so much charges on one person and lock him away for good unless he witness something. And, throughout my years, this is the worst I ever see."

Kevin was impressed by how close he was to figuring it out. "Well, in that case, you have a good idea what going on." Kevin eyes got closer to him.

"So… What if I tell you it have plenty corruption going on in the police service, you would believe me?"

The corporal hesitated. "Well, I can't deny it. But I was never in that. In fact, I get some superior officers in trouble when I just join the Service. That is one of the reasons why I is still a corporal at my age."

"Yeah, well, the only reason I standing here and talking to you is because of them kind of officers. The ones who would do anything and everything possible just not to get caught. They not working alone either. So it easy for them to pull it off."

The corporal seemed interested to hear everything that Kevin wanted to say.

"Alright, but what kind of corruption you talking about here?"

"Drugs…" Kevin said. The corporal didn't seem surprised and after a while he nodded in agreement.

"Okay, I wouldn't doubt it. It does have a lot of rumours going around that plenty of the top heads own drug blocks in different areas."

Kevin shook his head. "I wouldn't doubt the drug blocks either. But what I talking about plenty bigger than that. Is not just a simple block I talking about. Is a whole drug house."

The corporal eyes widened and he cleared his throat with a cough. He had a worried look on his face as if he wasn't sure whether he wanted to hear anything else about it. He worked his hands through his hair in a frustrated way and then glanced up and down the corridor to make sure there wasn't anyone eavesdropping on their conversation.

"Okay… I understand what you saying. But tell me something. How you manage to get tie up in all of this? I mean, from where it start?"

Kevin looked at him and studied whether there were any risks in telling him everything that he wanted to know. Then he reminded himself that they had deliberately altered his confession and because of that, he was scheduled for a lifetime behind bars.

No matter how personal his encounter had been, he knew it would be worth it to find that one person who would be willing to get their hands on the truth. It was then that he'd made up his mind to tell him all the important details from where it had all started to the moment they'd met at the hospital.

Kevin signaled him to come closer and he began to fill him in as quietly as possible.

During the conversation the corporal would stop him at certain points and check the corridor and the other prison cells to make sure they were not being overheard.

It took Kevin almost forty-five minutes to relive his experiences without being interrupted by any questions. When he was finished the corporal had left to check on his officers in the charge room and he'd returned about thirty minutes later with a cup of coffee and a large bottle of water which he'd given to Kevin. Kevin thanked him and started drinking the coffee while it was hot.

He just couldn't get a grip of it. Kevin allowed him that time to think.

When the coffee was finished Kevin crumpled the cup and threw it into the sink, and as if it was a cue, the corporal spoke.

"Right… I now remember where I know them officers at the hospital from." He seemed proud that he had collected his thoughts. "Them is ASP Ferdinand boys."

Kevin had no idea who he was speaking about, but he was glad that they were getting somewhere. Even if it meant he'd have to go to prison and someone in authority would be able to see the video sometime in the future, Kevin couldn't ask for anything more.

"He not easy though!"

"What you mean by that?" Kevin became a bit concerned.

"He have a lot of complaints filed against him of abusing his authority and he was on trial once for murdering two brothers. Nothing never come out of that, though."

"How come?"

The corporal looked at Kevin.

"The one and only State witness was murdered before the case did finish."

Kevin's eyes strayed from the corporal's. He was becoming worried. Not because of the murders but because of the fact that the ASP knew his way around the system. It was only then that he realized his stomach was starting to feel irritated by the coffee. He opened the bottle of water and took a long drink. It was like he'd been confident throughout the entire conversation until now. He was beginning to realize that he wasn't going up against any regular group of officers. They were possibly the most notorious within the service.

They were both quiet for a while.

"What about the other officers? You ever hear anything about them?"

"Yeah, I know the one with the tattoo on his neck too. Everybody know him. His name is Marlon Davis. He on suspension a few years now though."

Corporal Gibson was also looking disappointed with his results.

"That whole crew you talking about is ah set of rejects. No wonder they causing so much chaos."

Kevin could understand the corporal's concern now.

The place had gotten quiet for the longest time since they had started talking and although the corporal was standing right there his mind seemed distant. It was like he was already willing to give up before even attempting to help. He looked at Kevin with a face filled with regret and disappointment and then looked at the time on his watch.

"Yuh know, as much as I would like to help, you get yourself tie up in something real big here. You have no idea. Plus, the hardest working officers in Police Complaints couldn't stop them, much less a nobody like you, or a small fries like me. Sorry to say."

"Yeah, that might be true, but… that memory card is good evidence and all I really need is some kind of help to get it out there." Kevin stuck his hands through the bars as he pleaded with him.

"You don't understand. It not that simple. You would need all the help you could get…"

"I know, but you could help me. I would tell you where it is and you and some of yuh officers could get it and show it to somebody who could help."

"No." He shook his head. "That is not even a good

idea." Within that moment he quickly apologized and told Kevin that he wouldn't be able to get involved and started walking away.

"Yeah, but I need some kind of help. They going to put me away forever. I don't deserve this." Kevin said as tears started to fill his eyes. He cleared his throat.

As much as he wanted to shout out to the corporal, he'd maintain that respectable amount of privacy that they had shared earlier. The corporal was already at the beginning of the hallway.

"Corporal, I don't deserve this. I done plan to change my life… I swear." Kevin held onto the bars. "Corporal…?"

The corporal stopped.

"Corporal, please…"

The corporal stood there for a while and then he started walking again.

Kevin continued begging until the corporal's shadow and the sound of his footsteps had vanished from eye and ear.

Kevin sat on the floor. His face was already covered in tears and his eyes and throat were beginning to feel sore.

That was the first time since he had accepted the confession statement from the investigator that he had thought about what he had done. And the sudden change was because of thoughts of being separated from his unborn child.

He had given away his freedom and now Shantel and his baby would be the ones who'd have to suffer the consequence of living without him. It was a feeling that was destroying him from the inside out. A feeling that was making it hard for him to concentrate on anything else beside the baby's little face. Or at least what he believed their child would look like.

As time passed and silence filled the room, Kevin's mind drifted and he imagined himself holding his baby in his arms as Shantel stood in the kitchen preparing the bottle of milk. They both seemed happy and relaxed as they smiled at a joke that was said sometime before his imagination took him there. From there his thoughts went to his child as a toddler. Running and playing in the park with him giving chase. Shantel was lying on a picnic blanket a distant away, laughing at the way the little child was controlling Kevin's footsteps. It was a beautiful day, with big white clouds and blue skies.

Kevin came back to his present situation. He remembered yesterday morning having a similar atmosphere and then he realized that it wasn't just the day that was beautiful. It became obvious, that compared to everything he'd been through, he hadn't had a dull moment in the past. Circumstances would definitely make someone appreciate the littlest things in life, and although he might not have the opportunity to correct what he'd done wrong, he was appreciating the life he once had, more and more every second.

He opened his eyes, distracted by an odour that was circulating the room. It was the scent of all the previous prisoners that he hadn't yet got accustomed to. It was at its strongest every time air came through the vent.

Kevin got up and went to the bag taking out a change of clothes and then went to the sink to freshen up. When he was finished he returned to the bench.

The newspapers that covered the bench were now cold and the smell reminded him of a wet stray dog.

He removed as much as he could and threw it in a corner of the cell. He then used another set of clothes from inside the bag to spread on the bench like a blanket and lay down, hoping to get some rest until they were ready for him to organize for court in the morning.

Kevin heard someone calling his name and he turned around towards the bars.

He immediately sat up, surprised to see that the corporal was standing right there in front of him. The place was still dark, and he was a little disoriented, but because of his shoulders and joint pains from lying on the bench, he was sure that it wasn't a dream.

Kevin noticed that the cell gate was wide open and when his eyes met with the corporal's face he recognized that same concerned look that he had earlier when he'd figured out who the officers were.

Kevin had no idea what was taking place. Whether he was about to have his freedom, or the opportunity to talk to the person who could make it possible.

The corporal was quiet and hesitant, and he seemed as if he was having two minds about whatever he was deciding to do.

As much as Kevin wanted to say something he kept quiet, afraid that breaking the silence would cause the corporal to change his mind.

"You know," the corporal said after a few moments had passed. "You would never find another officer who willing to risk everything for a so-called criminal. And, to make matters worse, a stranger." The corporal slowly shook his head. "But no matter how hard I try to get this situation out of my head, it just there making me uneasy."

He was staring at Kevin straight in his face, and Kevin was trying to figure out exactly what the corporal had in mind.

The corporal turned to the open gate and then looked back at him.

"I going to help you get that footage in the right hands," the corporal said in a whisper, and there was already a trace of regret in his voice. "At the end of the day, is your choice. The gate open. All you have to do is go down this corridor here." He pointed to the corridor which was the opposite direction from the charge room.

"Don't worry, it have two cameras over yuh head, but none of them working."

Kevin looked at the gate and started to contemplate his choices.

"But, let me tell you something. Once you walk out that gate it not going to be easy. The service going to come after you with everything they have, from K9 to helicopters, and even soldiers."

The corporal waited a while, giving Kevin a chance to absorb everything that he had just said.

Kevin appreciated what he was doing and as much as he wanted to be free, he was worried about the corporal's safety.

"What about you?"

The corporal shook his head. "Don't worry about me. I in this thing long enough to know that shit happens.

You is ah important prisoner, but this is not the first time a prisoner escape, and it wouldn't be the last. Plus, I don't have long again to go. I retiring in three months time after thirty-three years of service."

Kevin felt a lot better. He started to think of all the bad things that could happen to him before retrieving the memory card.

He knew he had come a long way, but on the other hand he also knew what the corporal was saying was true, and once he decided to walk out of the station, he'd have to step up his game.

He was holding a piece of paper in his hand and he gave it to Kevin. Kevin opened it and saw a news reporter's name and the address for the news station which was located right here in Port-of-Spain. Kevin was familiar with seeing her appearing on the news.

"Me and Corbett-Smith is good friends from way back. I would call and tell she everything, so she would be expecting you. Just make sure and get that memory card, okay?"

"Yeah, okay."

Corporal Gibson gave him directions on how to reach the exit at the back of the station and reminded him that once he decided to leave there was only two possible ways that it would end. Either with him being killed, or with him getting the footage to the reporter who would broadcast it on live TV, and then there was no telling what would happen.

The corporal gave him a hundred-dollar bill and Kevin thanked him for everything and before leaving the cell he assured him that he would thank him again when everything was over.

He took all the corridors like the corporal said and when he had gotten to the metal door, he pushed it open and he could see the station's fence.

At that moment, he was afraid and excited to be free at the same time. But, above all, he knew he'd have to formulate a plan that would get him to the memory card and then to the news station without being caught. It would be his most difficult task, but he'd already made up his mind on not giving up.

Beyond the fence he could see the streets and buildings that he was somewhat familiar with. He stayed low and ran alongside the wall and made sure the opposite side was safe before climbing over.

As he walked through the streets he didn't see anyone for a very long time. The place looked deserted and there were hardly any cars passing by.

The first person he saw was a homeless man who was looking through a garbage bin for a meal. Kevin passed him and a few others without being noticed.

He was very alert as he walked and the one time he'd noticed blue flashing lights approaching from a distance, he hid himself between two buildings until they had passed by.

When he had gotten to the taxi stand, he got into the first vehicle that had agreed to take him to his apartment. He paid and pretended to be asleep throughout the entire drive, so he wouldn't be called upon for a conversation.

CHAPTER SIXTEEN

The time on the dashboard of the taxi read 4:26 a.m. and Kevin saw a lot of cars parked on the streets close to where he lived. He could also hear loud music as he approached. There was some kind of function or house party a couple streets down.

As he looked carefully, he could see people standing on the pavement in groups. Most of them looked like young persons and they were all dressed in party clothes. He told the taxi driver to drop him a few houses away and, only after looking around to make sure nobody was observing him or watching the building, did he start walking towards his apartment.

The volume of the music got lower the further he walked, but there were still a lot of cars on the street and in front of his driveway. He noticed a heap of rubble on the lawn. It was mostly the ceiling material and as he looked to the house he saw that the front door was replaced. He knew immediately that the landlord had taken it upon himself to start renovations.

As he walked unto his driveway he studied the area where he had collapsed after being shot. The lights were dim, making it difficult for him to notice if there were any bloodstains. His mind took him back to the morning it happened, and he could remember hearing the loud explosions and feeling pain about his body before falling to the ground. Without a second thought, he criticized the way he'd planned it and regretted the fact that he hadn't gone into the police vehicle instead and waited for a better opportunity.

He walked to the side window and looked inside. This was something he hadn't done the last time he was there. The glass was frosted from the dew and inside was very dark. He wiped the glass and took another look and he could see a lot of his belongings stacked inside of the room. He could almost see into the corridor.

He went to the door and turned the knob. It was open. Before entering he reminded himself of what had taken place and prepared his mind to deal with the flash-backs. He then pushed the door and entered.

There was a slight smell of gas and a lot of dust in the air causing him to cough uncontrollably until he pulled his jersey over his face, blocking his mouth and nose. He waved the dust away, trying to get a better view. He looked up and around. The entire ceiling was pulled down and debris was spread across the floor wherever he looked. All he could see overhead was the galvanize roof.

It seemed as though the workers were still in the process of renovating.

All of his furniture had been moved and the area where Wendell had died was nothing more than a memory. There wasn't any physical evidence connecting him to the past. Kevin thought this was a good thing, giving him a reason to move through the house without inviting guilt.

He kept fanning his hands through the air as he slowly walked towards the bathroom. He had to be extremely careful where he was placing his feet since there were a lot of screws and other sharp objects on the ground. His bedroom door was closed, and he stood there for a while studying whether he had just seen it like that through the window. He found it strange and the thought made him uneasy, but he quickly reminded himself of what he had come for. His eyes went to the bathroom door which was open and at that point nothing else was more important.

He heard the DJ interrupt the music to make an announcement and that was when he remembered it would be morning soon and the street would become crowded as everyone would be making their way towards their vehicles. By that time the station would learn of his escape and his apartment would be the first place they would look. He walked towards the bathroom door without wasting any more time.

Kevin opened his eyes in shock as he looked into the room. He was surprised and confused and then he raced in. He moved the jersey from over his face and the air was clearer than outside since the ceiling was still intact.

He couldn't stop staring at the empty spot where the shower curtain once was. The iron rod and curtain were now on the ground at his feet and he knew from the appearance of the room that the memory card was already gone. He took up the rod and checked anyway, finding nothing inside it. He separated the curtain and threw it outside the bathroom and still the memory card wasn't anywhere to be found.

He leaned against the wall, now out of ideas. It seemed as though his escape had been in vain. He started laughing to himself like a psychotic patient dwelling in his madness. A laughter that soon turned into tears and he began crying and went down to the ground.

Although he couldn't see the future, he became disappointed in himself for deciding to leave the cell. He knew that without the memory card his escape would only cause his death. There was no way around it. There was no way of proving to the country that he was being framed. There was just no hope.

He remained crying on the ground. He was seriously thinking about giving up.

He would either remain there until the officers arrived, or make his way to the nearest station where he would surrender in the presence of others, so he wouldn't be killed.

As time passed the music began distracting his thoughts. He sank his face into his arms, blocking off as much noise as he could.

A short time after he heard something like footsteps moving through the debris. He lifted his head and listened more carefully but nothing else was heard. He ignored it and started to think of the best way to accomplish the better one of his options.

There was another movement. He was sure of it this time. He got in position and crawled on his hands and knees to peek out the door. As his head went outside the room he saw a pair of boots coming towards his face. It'd happened so fast that he couldn't make a move. The kick sent him on his back and then the person ran into the room and started stomping and kicking him on his head and upper body. He tried to protect himself with his hands, but couldn't block all the areas at once.

The last thing he remembered was getting three stomps to his head and his head bouncing off the ground after each one.

Kevin felt something cold and wet splash unto his face and soak his upper body. As he gasped for air and struggled to open his eyes he saw a man walking away with a bucket in his hand. His head and shoulders pained badly. He couldn't even find the strength to keep his head up naturally for the first few seconds.

When he was finally able to look up, he saw several persons standing in front of him. The room was somewhat dark, making it difficult to see their faces. But he could see the sunlight coming through the space between the galvanize roof and the two-by-four. He realized that he was in a wooden structure, with two wooden windows that were both closed. Even the floor was constructed with wood. The sunlight was also penetrating through the creases around the windows and the sunlight from small holes on the roof was reflecting on the wall.

Kevin was on the ground in a corner of the room and his hands were tied behind his back. He could see his feet stretched out in front of him and they were tied together with rope. He couldn't move his lower body, only his head.

All the men were dressed in normal clothing. He didn't recognize any of them. He had no idea who they were working for either and that made it much more difficult to place them. They just stood there in silence as they waited for whoever had instructed them to wake him.

Kevin kept his head down while he waited and after a short while he heard the door open and someone entered the room. He lifted his head to observe the person's presence and as the person got closer he realized who it was.

He shook his head as Biggs stood in front of him.

Biggs was the last person he'd expected to see. He would understand if Biggs had captured him to retrieve his stolen items, but they were at his place and the memory card was missing. Kevin couldn't come to terms with why Biggs would want anything to do with the memory card.

Biggs slowly shook his head in disbelief and then looked back at his boys. Kevin already knew what he was thinking.

"Nah, this can't be real." Biggs laughed and walked away, and it was like he had to convince himself to walk back. He came closer to Kevin this time and studied his appearance, probably trying to come to terms with the fact that he was actually right there in front of him. Throughout that moment he had a worried look on his face.

"How on earth..." Biggs straightened up and shook away that thought.

"Who you working for? I really want to know. Since I know you, you working construction and liming with the wrong set of people. Always at the wrong place at the wrong time."

Kevin responded with a silent stare. He was confused by the type of question.

Biggs shook his head again. "Nah, you not that lucky and I know you is not no gangsta, so you have to be working for somebody, or with somebody."

Kevin could see that he was becoming impatient while he waited for an answer.

"I not working for anybody," Kevin said between his breaths. Biggs looked as if he was disappointed with Kevin's answer. He then laughed and put his hand over his mouth, still in disbelief that Kevin was in front of him. He shook his head and passed his hands through his hair.

"Why you fucking with me?" He sounded more frustrated than angry. "I know you and I know what you up against. It don't have no way on earth that one man could be so lucky. Plus, you is the last person I did expect them security to find in that house." He shook his head again and started pacing back and forth.

Kevin was weak and dehydrated. His throat felt parched and he was having trouble swallowing. Nevertheless, the word security played in his mind.

At that moment one of his boys walked into the room with a folded metal chair, and just when Kevin thought that things was about to get worst Biggs took it and sat down right where he was standing.

"What security you talking about?" Kevin said. His words sounding weak.

Biggs looked at him and smiled. "Me and you not that good yet. We might be in a little while. But not yet."

Kevin leaned his head against the wall and looked at

Biggs while he spoke. He was willing to do whatever it took so he wouldn't piss him off.

"You know what funny though? Karma is ah bitch." Biggs continued. "You and yuh so call team take something from me and the way it happen, I for one find that it was very disrespectful and I was willing to do anything just to get my stuff back. But…" He shrugged his shoulders. "Allyuh feel allyuh bad… and boldface." He paused and took a deep breath. "Now look what happen. Two people from yuh crew dead, and you get yourself tie up with the police. Who you going to turn to now?" Biggs remained quiet and kept his eyes locked on Kevin as if he was preparing to read his mind. Kevin felt intimidated and looked away.

Kevin knew his back was against the wall. He only had a few persons that he could trust, but even when united the few of them wouldn't be any match against the rogue police officers. It was just like the corporal said. They would be coming at him bigger and stronger than ever and if he wanted his plan to be successful, he'd have to get reinforcements also.

His eyes went back on Biggs, and like a child waiting to be disciplined he waited to hear what Biggs had to say. It didn't take long for Biggs to realize that he'd give in.

"I have a proposal for you," he said in a much lower voice.

"And what is that?" said Kevin.

"You have something that I want, and I have something that you need." Biggs stuck his hands into his pants pocket and pulled out something that he'd kept hidden in a closed fist.

Kevin was studying the expression on his face and trying to figure out if it was actually going to be that easy and that was when Biggs opened his hand and Kevin saw the memory card.

Kevin immediately felt a weight lift off his shoulders and he was amazed to see that the answer to all his problems was right in front of him.

Biggs leaned back on the chair and started explaining. "I went to yuh house some days after the police was there and me and meh boys turn that place upside down. It didn't take long before this come tumbling down with the curtain rod." He held up the memory card and started flipping it between two of his fingers. "When I see what it had on it and knowing that you was already in custody, I know it woulda only be a matter of time before you link with somebody to come back for it, and I was just waiting for that opportunity to get back my drugs."

Kevin turned and looked over his shoulder as he thought about everything that Biggs had said.

"Yeah, but how you even know I was there?" Kevin said and then turned back to him for the answer. He was hoping there wasn't another traitor in the crew.

Biggs slid his body to the edge of the chair and leaned closer to him. "Well, that was the easiest part. I pay a security unit to put in ah alarm and hide two cameras and they connect it right back to me. All I had to do after that was sit down and wait for one of allyuh to come back for this."

Kevin observed all the shadowed images in the room while Biggs kept his eyes on him. Although Biggs was not the type of person he would give his trust to. He was willing to work things out for the benefit of his freedom.

"So, what is the catch?" Kevin said.

Biggs shook his head. "It don't have no catch. It really that simple. I willing to put everything behind me. I just want back my business, and you could get this." He held up the memory card once more at an angle that Kevin could easily observe it.

Kevin bowed his head, trying to come to terms with what was being said. He then laughed at Biggs' expectations.

"So, you expect me to just call and tell Steve to bring back yuh drugs? And what? You think he would run and come?"

"I not sure how allyuh conversation would go, and I don't really give ah fuck what you tell him. Just do whatever you have to do for me to get it back. If you know you can't do that, let me know now so I wouldn't bother wasting my time. I would just do what I have to do."

Kevin started thinking again.

"Don't act like you don't want this." Biggs said in a calm voice. Kevin looked up at him again. "With the kind of information on this memory card, I know them officers wouldn't stop until they get rid of it."

Kevin was staring at Biggs as if his mind had drifted away. Now that Biggs knew the contents of the memory card, he also knew how much retrieving it meant to Kevin.

"Listen… Them drugs worth more than two million. And this eh worth nothing to me." Kevin looked at the memory card while trying to foresee how everything would play off. After some time had passed Biggs closed his fist and anxiously waited to hear what Kevin had to say.

Kevin remembered the altercation that took place at the club and then running through the bushes as they fired behind him with the intentions of killing him. He shook his head to himself. It was surprising how Biggs approach had changed drastically from then to now.

"So after everything that happen at the club. And after you try to kill me, you really want me to believe that you would put all that behind you now?" Kevin said.

"Yeah." Biggs shrugged. "That shouldn't be hard to believe. All of that did happen in the heat of the moment. I was just feeling so embarrassed and frustrated by the way everything went down." His hands kept moving as he spoke. "After allyuh beat me up and take my drugs allyuh still had the balls to shoot behind me and meh boys by that club. To me, that was just so fucking disrespectful. And at that point I didn't care about anything again. I just wanted to get back my business, even if I had to prove ah point by killing you and whoever else. Maybe even yuh whole team."

Kevin pierced his eyes at him. "Alright, so let we just pretend all this making sense." He paced his words in order to breathe freely and there were traces of pain and anger in his voice. "Before you say anything else, let me ask you something. That night when they take yuh stuff, you see me anywhere there?"

Biggs looked embarrassed by the question and Kevin knew that he and Sean had remained in the car which was parked a distance away making it difficult for Biggs to claim he saw either one of them, and making it easy for him to say he wasn't there, if he needed to.

"No. I wouldn't lie. I didn't see you, and that is the thing. It wasn't you I wanted. I wanted Steve. But you was the only person who was liming by yourself that whole night."

Kevin thought about what he'd just said and he remembered that Christine was Biggs's main source of information. It was now so obvious. From the moment she had snapped the pictures of both of them to the time she had received the message to leave. He lowered his head as he recapped the way it had played off.

"So, you was really the one who pay that girl to bring me in the car park?"

"Well…" The embarrassed look had left his face. "You don't have to make it sound like that. But yeah. She was part of it. It was strictly business though. And if it would make you feel any better, she didn't end up taking the money. Apparently it wasn't the right thing to do."

After seeing the look on her face as she ran to her car, Kevin knew she hadn't expected things to turn out that way. But, mentioning that she didn't take the money didn't make him feel any better. He felt foolish for not figuring her out sooner. He could've prevented a lot from taking place if only he had been observant.

"Listen, that whole night I was by myself for a reason." He was speaking louder than before, hoping to get his point across. "I didn't like what Steve do that night and I tell him about it. I tell him I didn't want anything to do with them again. The only reason I was by the club was because of Sean birthday lime and that was the last thing I was going to do with them."

"Okay. I wouldn't doubt it." Biggs looked convinced.

"And that was why I say, you was in the wrong place at the wrong time."

Kevin understood what he meant. He knew he should've never been at that party. Nevertheless, with everything that was being said, he was closer to making a decision.

"So what about yuh boys who get shoot?" Kevin said. "You willing to let that one slide too?"

Biggs lifted his eyebrow with a confused look on his face. "What you talking about? Nobody from my team did get shoot. We is top shooters. Allyuh can't even fucking shoot to save allyuh life. A set of wild shots all over the place like if allyuh have bullets to waste. One of we cars damage but that is small thing. We done replace that."

Kevin was staring at him as he realized he had gotten misleading information. Knowing now that no one from Biggs's crew was shot or injured, Biggs' intentions sounded convincing.

The room was quiet for a while and Kevin bowed his head and did some controlled breathing.

"So, now that we get all that out of the way. What going on? We have a deal, or what?"

Kevin didn't look up. He knew Biggs had the upper hand and saying no would no doubt piss him off more than he'd been in the past. He also knew that he wasn't in any position to negotiate, so he agreed.

Biggs smiled and after telling him that he'd made the right choice, he instructed one of his boys to untie him.

Kevin's hands and feet were untied within a few minutes and he quickly began to massage the sore spots where the rope had left a mark. He looked at Biggs, confused by his decision to let him loose even before receiving his drugs. Biggs caught his eyes and threw the memory card for him. Kevin caught it and began to examine it. He started getting flashbacks of his painful journey and couldn't believe that it was all for something so small.

Biggs stood up and two of his boys appeared at his side. Their faces were hard and expressionless. Kevin remembered one of their faces from the club's car park. He was the one who had brought him to his knees with the metal pipe. Their eyes made four and during that moment Kevin saw him grip the front of his pants waist making it known that he was carrying a firearm beneath his clothing.

"So," Biggs started saying. Kevin turned to him. "This is how we going to do this. You going to call one of yuh boys. I don't care who you call. Just call them and make arrangements for them to get my stuff. When they have it I would organize where we meeting and we would go there to finish this transaction. Once everything is everything, everybody would be free to go their separate ways. Even you. You understand?"

Kevin played it over in his mind and when he had no objections at the moment, he said he understood.

"Okay, good." Biggs opened his hand and was given a cell phone by the guy that Kevin didn't recognize. He then stepped forward and handed it to Kevin.

He looked at the time on his watch. "Is almost twelve o'clock. They have until three o'clock to get it and call back this number."

Kevin hesitated as he thought about who the better person to call was and what he was going to say. He then dialed the number of the cell phone Sean's cousin had left him with and Sean answered on the fourth ring. The phone was placed on speaker as instructed.

Kevin kept the conversation short as he explained what was taking place and what he needed him to do. He was sure to mention that it was a life or death situation. He wasn't in the position to answer too many questions, so he kept cutting Sean across by promising that he would explain everything when they met. When he had succeeded in the conversation, he hung up and handed the phone back to Biggs and they all left the room.

Later that afternoon when his boys had returned the sun had already moved across the room. One of the guys came over to Kevin and tied his hands together before taking him outside.

Kevin looked around, but the wooden structure was totally surrounded by bushes and trees and he couldn't see anything beyond that. They signaled him to get into a waiting pickup van and that was where they blindfolded him. Biggs was nowhere around.

There were a lot of turns and the road was very rough for most of the drive. Everyone in the vehicle remained silent and Kevin kept hoping and praying that everything would go smoothly.

About twenty minutes after the van came to a stop and all the doors opened and Kevin was pulled out of the vehicle. He could hear cars speeding nearby and he felt the warm afternoon breeze blowing against his skin. The blindfold was taken off and the first thing he saw was Biggs standing in front of him. Sean was on his knees and one of Biggs men was holding him by the collar with a gun to his head. His mouth was covered with silver tape and his face was angry though he looked unharmed. Kevin looked around.

They were standing in the ground floor parking of an old semi-constructed building. The walls were discoloured from passing time and the highway was less than a kilometre away. There were two cars behind Biggs and two additional men standing very close to him. Kevin didn't panic. He was angry.

His eyes went back to Biggs. "What going on? I thought we had ah deal.

"Well, I did always like them two words… Thought, and had!"

"Hmm." Kevin laughed in frustration and shook his head. "So, you saying we had a deal?" Kevin said while slowly nodding his head with a frown. He was secretly trying to pull his hands apart, but the ropes were too tight. If that wasn't the case, he would've surely jumped at Biggs and wrestle him to the ground and risked being shot.

"Yeah. We had ah deal."

"And what happen? What cause that to change?"

They were both distracted as Sean started moving around a lot and the man with the gun held on to his shoulder firmly. He took a moment to control him.

"What you think?" Biggs said in a loud aggressive voice.

"What? You didn't get all yuh drugs?"

"Yeah, I get every last ounce. Yuh boy here know not to play them kind of games with me."

"So what happen then?"

He shook his head in disbelief of what was being asked. "Why you acting like you don't have a clue how this thing does work? After everything that happen you expect me to just forget about all that?" He was looking at Kevin with pure hate in his eyes.

Kevin remained quiet. He was still twisting and turning his hands, trying to get them loose.

"We don't just forget about them kind of things." Biggs paused and shared his focus between Kevin and Sean. "But, it have three rules to this game. Play yuh cards right. Take what is yours and do whatever you have to do to get the fucking job done. Don't ever forget that." He stressed on his last words and his face was calm again.

He looked at the man who had the gun to Sean's head and with a flick of the risk the man helped Sean up and untied his hands. Sean hesitated and looked around before carefully pulling off the tape. Kevin was confused as to what was taking place.

One of the men on Kevin's side started untying his hands and when he was free he just stood there looking at Biggs in shock.

"Don't act surprised. I does always live up to my end of the bargain. I tell you what to do and you do it. So, at the end of the day, a deal is ah deal." The man next to Sean stuck the gun in his waist. He then went to one of the cars and got into the driver's seat.

"I just wanted to show you how easy it woulda be for me to kill two of allyuh. And imagine you going up against the whole police service. I hope you have a good plan. Judging from what happen here, you eh stand a chance. But I would leave them to handle you."

He started walking towards the car the man had gotten into and his boys followed. They all got in and the car started driving away slowly. The men on Kevin's side had also gone into the pickup van and started driving behind. Biggs's tinted window slowly went down, and he looked out as if he wanted to say something but didn't. They had simply driven away.

Kevin and Sean stood there studying each other for a while as if they were communicating in silence. Kevin then walked across to Sean and placed his hand on his arm.

"Good looking out bro," Kevin said in a saddened voice. His eyes filled with tears. He pulled Sean in for a brotherly hug and wiped away his tears. They were both thankful to be alive.

A few moments after, they both got into the remaining car which Sean had rented from a close friend and left.

CHAPTER SEVENTEEN

As they drove on the highway Kevin remained alert and observed as much as he could. The sky was becoming dark and he could see the sun setting in the rear-view mirror.

Sean was quiet, but it had taken him the last few minutes to convince Kevin that going to the hideout was their best option. The only problem was, Steve was presently there, and they'd be force to thrash things out now rather than later.

Sean continued to explain that after moving the drugs he had informed Steve of the deal that Biggs had made. And although Steve sounded most upset about it, Sean did what he believed was the right thing to do, regardless.

Kevin was impressed by all the possible risks Sean had taken. He had surely proven his loyalty to their friendship. Kevin studied him for a moment and then placed his focus on what was happening around them.

They'd eventually came off the main road and began heading through the tracks that led to the hideout. It had become a lot darker in the bushes and Sean brightened the headlights for a better view. Kevin remained quiet as he worked out the facts in the most necessary order.

There was only a short distance remaining and the thought of it made Kevin nervous.

"You okay?" Sean said, obviously noticing the way he was becoming tense.

"Yeah." He looked at Sean. "I good, I just hope he would understand."

"Yeah, well." Sean moved his eyes between Kevin and the road while speaking. "Don't worry about that. I was the one who move the drugs, so if he have to be mad at anybody most likely it would be me. But, whatever happen I would be right there with you from start to finish. So, just try and calm down. This is not something you should even be worrying about."

Kevin looked away and smiled at his response.

A few minutes after they pulled up at the hideout and Sean switched off the engine and came out. Kevin slowly followed.

As they walked to the door Kevin became distracted and as he looked to the roof he noticed the dazzling light from the burning lamp.

Sean knocked and called out to Steve and waited for him to come to the door. The wait was more intense than expected and Kevin felt his heart racing against his chest as his thoughts slowly faded away.

The door opened slightly, and Kevin noticed Steve's shadow as he walked back into the house. Sean looked back at him before pushing the door and going inside. Kevin cautiously followed.

On the inside Steve was seen sitting on the couch with his face buried in the palm of his hands. He had gotten a lot smaller from the last time Kevin had seen him at the hospital. They both stood there as if they were waiting for the other person to start talking. Sean wasn't taking the hint, so Kevin broke the silence.

"What going on bro?" he said nervously and looked at Sean who used his hands to encourage him to continue. "Listen, I know you must be vex with me and mightn't even want to talk. But, in case I don't get a chance to say anything else, I just want to apologize for what happen."

It was like his last words had triggered a reaction as Steve slowly lifted his head. His face bore no expression.

"Sorry for what? What you sorry for?"

Kevin looked at Sean and his expression showed no hint to the question.

"Well, for making Sean go behind yuh back and take the drugs. I know that was real outta timing."

"Oh." Steve slowly nodded with his mouth turned upright as if he was disgusted by everything that had taken place. His mind seemed distant. "So, if you sorry for taking the drugs, how I suppose to feel?" He leaned back on the couch while looking at the two of them. Kevin didn't answer. "How I suppose to feel knowing that I is the one responsible for dragging all of allyuh in this mess?"

Kevin remained quiet. He had worked out a lot of scenarios while on his way here, but he hadn't expected this type of reaction from Steve.

Steve shrugged his shoulders for an answer, but hadn't

gotten any.

"Okay, don't answer that." his eyes fell to the ground for some seconds and then came back to them. "How I suppose to even feel to know two people dead all because of me and my foolishness?"

Again, there was no answer. Steve shook his head and the room was quiet for an awkward amount of time. He then joined them on their feet. Kevin noticed he wasn't standing as straight as he normally did.

"Listen, I not going to continue like this." He started moving across the room. Kevin noticed that he was now walking with a limp and his upper body was slightly bent to the right because of the injury to his spine. Steve stopped and looked back at them. His face was now sad. He took a moment to control his emotions before speaking.

"I coulda end up just like Marcus and Wendell," he said in an angry voice. Kevin wasn't offended by his tone since he knew Steve was angry because of his situation and not at either one of them. Steve took a deep breath and gathered his thoughts.

"I want allyuh to understand something. Especially you." His eyes were on Sean. Sean's face brightened up and he became more attentive. "When you call me earlier today and tell me what you was about to do, I was angry, but ah wasn't angry because you take the drugs. I was angry that you take it without talking to me first. I don't trust Biggs. I didn't care if you did take all the guns and money too. I just didn't want anything to happen to any one of allyuh. I don't know how I woulda live with that burden." He paused and studied their faces for a moment before continuing. "Look at me. I can't even walk properly. But, I still glad to be here. I know I still here for a reason and I not going to fuck it up this time." He was looking directly at Kevin now. "Listen, after we help you straighten out this mess. I don't want anything to do with guns or drugs again."

Kevin looked at Sean and there was a proud look on his face. Kevin felt the same way. He was extremely glad to hear Steve talk like that.

Steve started walking towards them with his hands stretched out and the three of them wrapped their hands across each other's shoulders and embraced what remained of their friendship. When they had loosened their grip, Steve held on to Kevin's hand as if he was about to give him a handshake.

"Congratulations," Steve said.

Kevin looked into his eyes, confused to what he was talking about. "Congratulations for what?"

Steve smiled at the question. "Congratulations on having yuh first child."

Kevin lifted his eyebrows and his eyes opened up. He pulled away his hands and placed them over his mouth overcome by joy, as he regained a feeling of worthiness. He had no idea that he was already a father.

He turned, thinking about it and thanking God for making him experience such a milestone, even with all the conflict that surrounded him. He looked at Sean, wondering why he hadn't told him about it earlier, but Sean simply lifted his hands in defence mode indicating that the news was also new to him.

"When she make baby? And what I get? A boy, or a

girl?" He was overwhelmed and anxious, and there were just so many questions he wanted to ask.

"You get a girl. She born last night. And that is one of the main reason I was so worried when Sean call. I didn't want nothing to happen to you, especially now that you get yuh daughter."

Kevin sighed and looked to the roof. The attempt wasn't enough to hold back the tears that filled his eyes. He turned and walked away. Sean was sitting on the hand rest of the couch.

From the moment Shantel had gotten pregnant Kevin had always prayed for a baby girl and now his prayers were answered.

He tried his best to control his emotions and then thanked Steve for sharing such great news.

"How you find out?" Kevin was curious.

"Well, when you was in hospital she call me and tell me that she was going to check you, but I tell she no. I tell she to wait until we know for sure what was going on. And when Sean tell me about the drug house and the memory card, that was when I tell she not to go and visit you until after the court case. She call me Friday morning and tell me she was going into labour, and then she call me last night and tell me she did get a girl."

"Alright, cool... So, you tell she about the drug house?"

"No." He shook his head. "I didn't tell she anything about that. I just tell she that we not sure what going on with you, and is best she don't get involve until after the case."

"Okay." Kevin was smiling. He knew it would be a

task to cope with everything, but he also knew that he'd have to pull himself together and accept reality.

Steve returned to his seat and gave Kevin a few more minutes to himself before asking him to explain everything that was going on between him and the police officers in details. Sean was also anxious to get the full story since they hadn't spoken about it in the car.

Kevin pushed his hand into his pocket and pulled out the memory card. They both leaned forward to get a good look at it.

"This is what everything is about." He handed it to Steve, and Steve quickly examined it and passed it to Sean. "That is what they after," Kevin said and started explaining everything that happen. When he was finished they both seemed surprised by what he'd been through. They took a few more minutes to absorb everything that was said.

"So," Steve said while holding the memory card. "We have to try and get this to the news reporter woman before the police get it?"

"Yeah, but not try. She have to get it."

"Yeah, well. That is what I mean," Steve said without taking his eyes off the memory card. He was anxious to view the contents, but accepted the fact that there wasn't anything to play it on.

Steve stood up and Kevin took the memory card and pushed it back into his pocket. "Okay, time to figure out how we going to do this," Steve said, and they began brainstorming and voicing their suggestions.

They managed to go at it for a little over an hour and it was Sean's idea that sounded most workable.

His cousin Keisha had done a few courses in cosmetology before becoming a nurse. Sean would contact her tomorrow morning and bring her to the hideout in order for Kevin to get a Rastafarian disguise which should help them evade the police. If that didn't work, Steve would be following in another car and he'd cause a distraction which would take the officers off route and away from the news station, giving Sean and Kevin enough time to get there and give the memory card to the reporter. It was the perfect plan and they all agreed on it.

The next thing was to decide who would be carrying a firearm, and as much as Kevin didn't want to, it had come down to Steve and himself, since Sean continuously refused.

They were satisfied with their accomplishments, and it was already after midnight and they needed their rest. Steve and Sean shared the bed and Kevin remained on the couch.

There was a lot on his mind and it took him a while of twisting and turning and being distracted by the noisy insects before he'd managed to put his mind at ease.

He woke up to a woman's voice and as he sat up his neck and shoulders ached. He noticed Steve, Sean and Keisha standing close to the door with a laptop resting on the counter in front of them. Sean noticed him before anyone else, then Steve and Keisha looked on.

"Aye, look who finally wake up." Sean said in a teasing manner. Keisha raised her hand and acknowledged him.

Kevin got up and walked over to them while using

his hands to message his shoulders. The pain didn't ease.

"What going on Keish?" he said when he had gotten close enough and greeted her with a hug. He felt somewhat embarrassed by everything she might've heard about him. She was dressed in blue jeans and a white blouse, and her expensive perfume lingered in the air.

"What? No work today?"

"Yeah, I have to be there for four. It nice to actually see you again with all these rumours going around."

"Hmm, I could imagine." He looked at the laptop and saw officers with guns on two of the twelve blocks of cameras. He tried to observe their faces, but her laptop screen wasn't big enough.

"This is some real corruptive shit you have here," Steve said, and his words brought everyone's eyes back to the screen. Kevin noticed the date being, 16.05.2012 and the time was 9:18 p.m. Kevin realized that, that was two days before he had gotten there.

"What happen so far?" Kevin asked. Everyone looked at him in a curious way.

"Wait? What happen? You eh watch it yet?" Sean said, and everyone was anxious for the answer.

"No. I just watch ah small piece and when I see two people get shoot I take it. I eh get chance to watch it out yet."

"Oh, okay," Sean said, and their eyes went to the screen again. Keisha pressed a button and it started to fast-forward.

"Well," Steve started explaining. "So far the video start off on the thirteenth. That was a Sunday. Nothing didn't happen until Tuesday. That was when the soldiers bring in the drugs. The workers come in Wednesday morning and in less than half-an-hour they went upstairs and start stripping and then come back downstairs to start cutting and packing the drugs."

Kevin would momentarily glimpse at the screen to see if anything was taking place while it was moving fast, but there wasn't anyone but officers on the screen.

"On Wednesday and Thursday they had them working some long hours without any break. They start to work around eight, and finish around eight, nine. Three people dead within them two days."

"What?" Kevin was shocked. He wrapped his hands behind his head and asked why.

"One person try to get high when he thought nobody was looking, and the other person try to make a run for the door," Keisha answered without looking away from the screen.

Kevin glimpsed at the screen and notice that all the workers were upstairs getting naked and they were then led downstairs by three armed officers. There were more officers waiting downstairs. The video was still moving fast.

"And why they killed the third person?" Kevin asked. Sean and Steve looked at Keisha with sad faces, waiting for her to answer. She gave him a silent stare.

"I would show you just now. I wouldn't be able to explain that one."

Kevin became concerned upon hearing her answer.

"I don't think they from Trinidad though." Steve interrupted.

"Why?" Kevin asked.

"I not really sure. I just saying," Steve continued. "I watching the complexion and their appearance. I feel is some kind of Spanish link they have."

"Hmm," Kevin observed a few of the workers and realized what Steve was saying could be true.

On the screen he saw one of the workers being pulled away from the metal table and that was when Keisha pressed play and they all quietly observed what was about to take place.

Kevin noticed three of the officer surrounded the male worker and they all started kicking and stomping him as he pleaded for mercy. After almost three minutes of beating one of the officers handed his firearm to another officer and took out what looked like a combat knife. He kneeled next to the worker and stuck the knife into the man's throat and they all watch as his life leaves his body.

Kevin turned away, disgusted by the way they had treated another human being. Keisha started fast-forwarding it again and Kevin walked over to the couch. At that point the remainder of the video wasn't important to him. All he could think about was getting it to the reporter, so all the officers involved would be dealt with accordingly.

The three of them stood there for a little more than twenty minutes and when the video was finished Sean confirmed that there had been another death, bringing the total to five.

"And what happen to all the other workers?" Kevin asked from where he was sitting on the coach.

"Well," Steve started saying. "We just see them put on their clothes and leave in one of the army trucks. I not sure what happen after that."

Kevin was a bit shaken up by what he saw and heard.

"You still want to know what happen to that third person?" Keisha took his attention. As much as Kevin knew it might be as gruesome as what they did to the man with the combat knife, he got up and walked across to the laptop.

Keisha pressed play and walked over to the couch where Sean was now sitting.

Kevin noticed the date was 16.05.2012, and the time was 1:24 a.m. As he looked on, he could see several officers in the main room upstairs. Some of them were standing and some were sitting, but they were all wearing nothing more than their underpants. Two of the officers went to the door of the room that Kevin had slept in and knocked on the door. When the door was opened, both officers made their way into the room and came out with one of the female workers. They then closed the door behind.

The woman was screaming and kicking as they threw her on the couch and two other officers joined in and they'd all started ripping off her clothing.

Kevin turned his head and told Steve to take it to the end. Steve fast-forwarded it and then called out to Kevin. Kevin saw an officer getting off the woman's lifeless body and started putting his pants back on while the other officers watched.

Kevin could feel the rage building inside him as if he was about to explode. His hands made a fist and he shouted out and punched the nearest wall. His hand bounced off and he could see blood on his knuckles. He leaned against the wall and allowed his body to slide to the floor. He buried his face in his hands and started crying. He couldn't stop thinking about the mess he'd gotten himself into, and after seeing those video footages he realized now more than ever how lucky he was to be alive.

He heard footsteps approaching and noticed Keisha's feet next to him. She then kneeled beside him and placed her hand on his arm.

"Listen, I know yuh upset, and I know it don't have nothing I could say right now to change that. But, just know I come here because I believe you didn't do none of them things they talking about, and I glad I get a chance to see for myself. The same way the whole country would see when you carry it to the news station."

She gently massaged his arm and then lifted his chin. His eyes were blood-red, and his face was wet with tears. She stretched out her hand and Steve handed her a handkerchief which she used to dry his face and then wrapped it around his knuckles.

"Come!" She stood up while holding his hand. "Let me give you yuh makeover." He started getting up. "You wouldn't even recognize yourself when I finish with you, I promise."

She led him to the couch and took out the fake dreadlocks and other cosmetics from her bag. Steve stood and watch as she created her masterpiece.

Sean was over at the laptop making a few copies of the memory card.

Keisha took an hour and a half to cut, glue and dye his new dreadlocks and beard. When she was finished she handed him a mirror and he had put it to his face to see the new look that had Sean and Steve so amazed.

Kevin's eyes lighted up and he stood to his feet, surprised at what he was looking at. He looked totally different and she was so right when she said he wouldn't be able to recognize himself. He smiled and pulled her in for a hug, lifting her off her feet. She was beyond talented. He brought the mirror to his face again and carefully examine his new Rastafarian look, with black and cocoa brown dreadlocks and patched beard.

With his new look he had no doubt that their plan was going to work.

He thanked her again and when she noticed the time she reminded them that she had to leave for work.

Her car was parked at the main road to draw less suspicion. She quickly organized her belongings and left with Sean and Steve. They would rent two vehicles and Steve would go ahead of them to observe their most reliable route and remain at a static location. Sean would return for Kevin who should be ready and waiting at that time.

Sean had returned at 5:15 p.m. and Kevin was already dressed in one of Steve's blue jeans, a long sleeve shirt and a tie. Sean took twenty minutes to get dressed in a jeans and short sleeve shirt.

"You ready?" Sean said as he walked into the room bringing Kevin back to reality. Kevin stood up and Sean handed him two copies of the memory card as he'd requested. Kevin hesitated for a moment.

"What happen? You good?"

"Yeah… Kinda." Kevin couldn't stop thinking about his daughter and he was becoming anxious to see her.

"I know it might be kind of risky, but I want to see

them before we go."

"See who?" Sean looked concerned.

"Who else? Shantel and meh daughter."

Sean shook his head and mumbled, "This can't be happening now," to himself.

The truth was, they both knew there was a strong possibility of things working out. But, if it didn't, the next time Shantel would be seeing him would be to identify his body at the morgue. The plan was mostly Sean's idea and although they had time on their hands they were working as a team and with a schedule. A schedule that catered all remaining time for unforeseen circumstances.

Sean thought about it for a while and then agreed. They both left the house and got into the new sedan that Sean had just rented. Sean started the engine and drove out onto the street. He'd decided that he'd only contact Steve and inform him of the change of plans if they were running behind time.

Along the way they saw police officers and soldiers patrolling the streets in vehicles and some on foot. But, lucky for them, no vehicles or persons were being questioned or searched.

The streets were quiet and deserted, and it had taken them twenty-five minutes before they pulled up a few houses away from Shantel's parents place.

Kevin had gotten a phone from Sean and he'd contacted her when they were about to leave so she would be expecting him. He also told her about his Rastafarian disguise. He called again when the vehicle had come to a stop.

Sean left the engine running and they kept scanning

their surroundings.

Kevin saw her look out her bedroom window and then the front door opened a few moments after and he saw when she stepped back into the house.

Sean drove up to the house and Kevin made sure it was safe before exiting the vehicle and making his way into the yard. He noticed her father's car parked in the driveway and he walked past it and went into the house.

When he entered Shantel was standing by the door and it was as if she needed to take a moment to recognize him. She signaled for him to be quiet and closed the door behind them. She then held his hand and led him through the dark house and into her bedroom.

The light in her room was dim and he could see his daughter sleeping on a smaller blanket on the bed. He walked closer, admiring her for a moment. She was lying on her side in a pink and white suit. She was a beautiful brown-skinned baby with pink lips and curly hair. He remembered Shantel describing what she believed their baby would look like and she was right about the complexion and the curly hair. He knew if things were going smoothly she would've had her opportunity to brag about it. And she'd have every right to. Shantel came to his side and gripped his hand tightly.

It was like neither one of them could believe they were standing in each other's presence again. He turned to her and she was just standing there looking at him. She saw beneath his new appearance. She saw him as the person she knew him to be. He couldn't hold back his emotions and tears settled in his eyes. He realized that her eyes were already red and puffy.

Within that moment Kevin leaned into her and took her in his arms. He held her tight and he could feel her breathing against his neck. He enjoyed feeling her warm body in his arms again and he wished he didn't have a reason to let go. It was as if she'd read his mind as she tightened her arms around him. He could feel their heartbeats slow and got into one rhythm as his body became calm and he felt as if a weight was being lifted away. His stomach pushed out short gasps of air and he started sobbing. After everything he'd been through, she was the only person who brought him to a peaceful state of mind.

They stood there for a couple minutes.

"I miss you so much," she said. He leaned away and looked at her. He noticed a streak of tears working its way down her cheeks and he wiped it away and when he got his words together he told her he missed her even more. She pulled him back into her arms.

"Look how things change. I does think about it all the time and it just so sad... How we even end up like this?" she said.

He thought about everything she'd been going through and he realized that there wasn't a good enough answer that would replace the pain.

"I sorry babe," he said in a soft voice as tears ran down his face. "I so sorry."

He held her face between his hands and looked into her eyes.

"I would make it up to you, I promise."

Her eyes became concerned and she pulled her face away from him and walked away at the same time.

"How?"

He studied the way her attitude had suddenly changed and then he said that he was going to fix it.

"How you planning to fix it?" she said in a more aggressive but concerned voice. It was her stare that demanded an answer.

Kevin started to think things through as she stood there anxiously waiting to hear what he had to say. He hadn't told her about the drug house, and he realized leaving out that piece of information was coming back to haunt him now. As much as he'd like to fill her in, time was becoming a disadvantage to him.

He quietly shook his head and looked at her with a face that was requesting her forgiveness.

Her crying became more intense and she sat on the bed and sank her face into her hands. He sat next to her and when he attempted to move her hand she pulled away. He pleaded for her forgiveness a couple times and then he eventually held her around her arms and pulled her closer to him. He kept her there until she was calm. She then lifted her head and looked at him for his explanation and he waited a while before speaking.

"Babe, you have to understand, is not what you thinking," he said.

She shook her head in a frantic manner and began massaging her forehead in frustration.

"So, what it is then Kev?" Her voice sounded sore and she cleared her throat. "I does watch news and read papers, every single day, from the day the shooting happen to now..." She looked up at him expressing her anger at everything that he'd put her through.

"Look how long I begging you to stop hanging out

with them fellas and you just keep getting yourself tie up in more and more shit. Look how far it reach now... What you could possibly tell me? And how you really planning to fix this, Kevin? You tell me?"

Kevin looked at her without saying a word. At this point he was willing to tell her everything but didn't know how or where to start.

"Go ahead. I waiting to hear how you going to fix this. And, while you at it, tell me how you planning to bring back the dead too?" Her face was serious.

Kevin got up and slowly walked across the room as he began studying everything she had just said.

It was the first time he realized that without the video footage, he had no story. The officers had done a good job in making believers out of every citizen, even her. And he had never once responded to refute their claims. And, to make matters worse, he had agreed to having committed all the crimes and that had already gone public.

He started thinking about his contact and wondered how she'd react to him. As much as he tried to convince himself that everything would go smoothly, he couldn't imagine her willingly sitting down and having a discussion with him, knowing very well that it was the second time he had become one of the country's most wanted criminal in just a few months.

He became skeptical that their plans would work, and it was the first time he was looking at it from that angle.

He began wondering if he should even go through with it.

He heard her footsteps and could feel her presence

behind him.

"Kevin..."

He turned around and looked at her. She was standing right behind him. There were still traces of tears on his face and he'd only managed to wipe it away after she'd noticed.

She was staring at him as if she was trying to get a good look at the person she once knew. The person he was beneath the Rastafarian disguise and without all those accusations.

"Babe... I really don't know what going on," she said. "But, if is one thing you should know is that I love you, and I would never give up on you." She tried to control her feelings by turning away for a second and when she looked back at him he realized tears were running down her cheeks again.

"I don't know how I manage to make you change this much without trying harder to put a stop to it," she continued. "And right now, you change so much. I don't know if is for revenge, or whatever. But you is not the same person I know. And, I wish you did never meet Steve or any of them fellas. I really missing the old you. The person you was two years ago." She slowly shook her head in disappointment.

Kevin was looking into her eyes and he didn't turn away until she had finished saying what she had to. He knew she was wrong about him changing but he also knew that he hadn't given her a reason to think otherwise, so he wasn't in any position to blame her.

His eyes moved around the room. He wasn't sure how to respond, and there was a lot of thoughts going through his head.

She held him in her arms and they stood there embracing each other. Afterwards he was the one who led her back to the bed and they both sat down and he started telling her about the corrupt officers, the drug house, what he had seen and what they were after. When he was finished explaining she was at a loss for words and upset that she was now finding out. He went on to apologize for not telling her about it sooner and said it was because she was pregnant, and he did not want to stress her out.

He started telling her that it was Sean who was waiting outside and before he could get further his phone began ringing. He ignored it and he could see that she was worried about who it might be.

It rang a second time just when he was about to continue talking and he decided to get it out of his pocket and answer the third time it rang.

It was Sean—there was a police vehicle patrolling the area, he told Kevin, and he had to make a block in order not to create any suspicion.

Kevin walked to the window and he looked outside just in time to see the blue lights at the bottom of the street. He studied the vehicle for a while before moving away from the window and he was looking in Shantel's direction when he told Sean to give him five more minutes before returning for him.

Shantel looked disappointed that he was about to leave again. His thoughts were different though. He was debating whether to continue the conversation or not. Then he realized he had no choice. If it was his desire to be with them again, he'd have no choice but to leave before the officers return.

He felt committed to continue the conversation but instead he went right to apologizing for everything.

She looked at him, trying to figure out what he was about to do and that was when she'd joined him on his feet.

"You still didn't tell me how you planning to fix it, Kev."

Kevin was quiet. He knew if he told her of the plan, she would become worried.

"How you planning to fix it?" she asked again. She held on to his hand and tried to pull him back to the bed. He wasn't allowing her strength and emotions to overcome him.

He handed her a copy of the footage and told her to watch it and she'd understand everything that was going on. At that moment she became sad and she put more effort in her attempts to pull him back towards her.

He heard Sean pull up outside the house.

"Babe, listen to me… Kev?" she said while pulling on his arm. Her strength couldn't be compared to his. She continued.

"Come nah babe, we could figure this out. You don't have to go!"

He left the room and headed for the door. He knew although Shantel had no idea what he was up to, she wasn't going to give up on him that easy. He'd have no choice but to be strong for the both of them.

"Kev, Kevin… Baby." She continued pleading with him. "Whatever you going to do baby, you don't have to do it. My friend know somebody from Venezuela. I could talk to somebody." He was right in front of the door and he reached out and opened it.

He hated seeing her this way, but as much as it was destroying him inside he knew he was too close to give up now.

"Baby?" she said in her most affectionate voice. A voice he'd never built the courage to ignore. He looked at her.

They were both on the porch and she was keeping her voice down. She clearly knew if she caused a commotion it would attract unnecessary attention from her parents and neighbours and it would only make matters worse.

He turned to her and he could see that look in her eyes as if she was losing something she was prepared to die for.

He looked to the street and noticed that Sean was looking right back at him.

He closed his eyes and took a deep breath and that was when he realized he'd have to disappoint her. Out of everything that he'd been through, seeing her like this wasn't making things any better. It was obvious that she was being torn apart and their relationship was something she was willing to die for. He loved her more than words could explain, and he was willing to sacrifice everything just to see her happy.

He relaxed his arms and looked at her for a minute and when she realized he wasn't putting up a fight she released his hand and began telling him about her friend with the Venezuelan connections.

Kevin wasn't as interested as he looked. He was more focused on what he was about to do and the reaction he was going to get from her.

"Shantel?' he said in a soft voice and she became quiet and looked at him. His stomach felt cold.

"I sorry," he continued. "But, I have to go. I have something I need to take care of." She stopped and just stared at him with a worried face.

Kevin went into the car and Sean drove off at once.

CHAPTER EIGHTEEN

It was 6:50 p.m. and Kevin remained in the backseat as Sean got on to the highway. He'd decided to sit at the back so that if things didn't go as planned, Sean would say he was only the driver who was hired by the disguised Kevin. It was the easiest way for him to deny having any affiliation with Kevin.

They made their way onto the northbound lane where there were a lot of cars on the highway. Only a few of them could keep up with Sean's speed of 140 km.

Kevin hung up the phone that Sean had handed to him and threw it to his side. He looked into the rear-view mirror and his eyes met with Sean's.

"What he say?" Sean said. Kevin was still distracted by the information he'd just gotten from Steve. He had a worried look on his face as he pulled the gun from his waist, chambered a round and kept it in his hand. He was hoping he wouldn't have to use it.

"What he say?" Sean said in a voice which was much louder and demanding than before.

Kevin hesitated before answering.

"He say it have plenty police on the shoulders," Kevin said with concern. "But the first roadblock is on the Beetham."

"What about passing on the bus route or the main road?"

Kevin shook his head. "Apparently there worse."

Sean got quiet for a short time before asking if Steve was already in position. He looked relieved on hearing the answer.

Sean turned left and went onto the westbound.

The sun entered the car and Kevin turned his head to the side, protecting his eyes. Sean pulled down the sun visors.

They continued driving for a few more minutes and Kevin noticed that vehicles were slowing down ahead. They both looked at each other, knowing very well that this was what it was all about. Both the day and their anticipation were coming to an end and they would soon know if tomorrow would bring forth a brighter day. Either way, they weren't about to turn back now.

The place was becoming dark and as they got closer to the cars Kevin could see a group of police officers and soldiers standing guard while the others were scanning through the incoming vehicles.

There were also a lot of officers and soldiers on the eastbound lane doing the same.

The actual officers who were asking the occupants of the vehicles to present their documents were standing at the beginning of the stop.

Kevin kept his head straight while trying to identify

the car that Steve was in. To his surprise, he wasn't anywhere in sight, or at least he hadn't noticed him.

They were only one car away from the search. There were four occupants in the car in front of them and Kevin noticed that the officers were observing each one carefully. There was an officer on either side, shining their lights into the car, looking for anyone with the slightest resemblance to their escapee. Little did they know, there was a possible chance that their search could soon come to an end.

After several minutes the officers confirmed their satisfaction with one another and they allowed the car to proceed without any further interrogation. Another officer who was standing in front with two soldiers directed Sean to drive towards them.

Kevin saw that Sean was looking at him in the mirror again and Kevin whispered to him, telling him to remain calm.

Those few seconds became intense and Kevin's stomach felt heavy and his nervousness was starting to affect his breathing.

The gun was still in his hand and he was holding it so tight that his hand was beginning to turn numb. He kept it as close to his side as possible.

All the windows in the car were already down and the officer on Sean's side started walking towards him. On reaching a safe distance he began shining his light into Sean's face and around his body. After observing him for a few seconds the officer walked closer and asked him to present his documents.

The officer on Kevin's side was assisting another officer in observing the documents of the driver adjacent to them.

Kevin's body was becoming tense. He could hardly focus, and his only hope was that Sean would be able to drive them out of the shooting if that was what it came down to.

Kevin noticed Sean's hands were shaking as he unbuckled his seatbelt and stretched across to the glove compartment to locate his wallet and the insurance.

At that moment the officer asked who the car belonged to and Sean hesitated to answer. Kevin remained quiet in order to keep the focus away from him.

"Switch off the vehicle," the officer instructed and kept the light on Sean, carefully studying his movements. The officer's hand was already on his firearm.

The other officer realized that something was taking place and came walking towards Kevin. He too began shining his light from a distance and kept his hand on his firearm.

The engine was cut off and Kevin observed how much they were outnumbered and stuck the gun beneath his leg.

The officer was right outside his door now.

"What going on here?" the officer said to his colleague and he briefed him on the situation. He then shone his light into the car and around Kevin before asking where they were coming from.

Kevin attempted to look up at him but all he could see was the bright white light, nothing else. He felt a bit relieved that the officer hadn't recognized him.

"Mount Hope," Kevin said, with confidence and

loud enough for Sean to hear, in case he was asked a similar question.

"And where you from?"

Kevin begin thinking of anywhere outside and as far away from Chaguanas as possible. The light was affecting his eyes and he twisted his face expressing his discomfort to the officer. His actions bought him some time.

"Couva." It was the only place that had come to his mind due to the light being a major distraction and everything else that was taking place around him. Plus, Chaguanas and Couva both began with the letter 'C'. That was as far as his memory took him.

The officer was studying Kevin's face for a while and then he asked him to present his ID card.

Sean had just handed over his driver's permit and insurance to the officer on his side and he was just sitting there waiting for further instructions. Kevin pretended to be looking through his pockets but was actually working up a reason why he couldn't present his ID card. During his arrest his fingerprints were the only thing that had connected him to his name.

He knew not having his ID card during a road exercise this big would not be ignored and they could become victims of a prolonged interrogation.

After making a lengthy search, he mentioned to the officer that he was in a hurry and it was possible that he had forgotten his wallet at home. The officer looked displeased and after thinking for a while he walked back to an officer in a khaki suit and Kevin saw them exchanging words.

Kevin looked at the time and it was 7:13 p.m. He

became anxious and annoyed that they were already running late.

His eyes went down to the phone and he saw that there were twelve missed calls. It was only then that he realized Sean had put the phone on silent for some unknown reason. The phone started lighting up again and as he opened it up he realized it was Steve and he answered.

"You know how long I calling allyuh?" Steve said. "Get ready to move, I coming through on the shoulder."

Kevin looked into the rear-view mirrors and then spun around but didn't see anything out of the ordinary. He then looked over his shoulder and saw that the officer was observing his actions. The officer started walking towards him, shouting at him to end the call. Before Kevin could react he heard a loud crash and at that instant, shots began firing.

Officers were scampering for safety and the soldiers quickly began firing back at Steve's vehicle that had burst its way through the roadblock and sped away.

When Steve had gotten too far, all the soldiers and officers ran towards their vehicles and started to give chase, leaving all the cars in the roadblock unattended.

Sean turned and looked at Kevin in confusion and only when Kevin had shouted at him to drive the car, he started the engine and drove away leaving all the other drivers puzzled by what had just taken place.

By the time Sean had made his way into Port-of-Spain Steve had already led the officers far away. Sean drove through the two orange cones that were used as a checkpoint barrier at the news station's car park.

The security had attempted to stop them, but they'd ignored him, pulled into a parking spot and quickly made their way into the building.

There was another security behind the desk in the lobby where Kevin and Sean quickly scanned the notice board for directions around the building.

"Who allyuh come to?" the security said and when he got no answer he got up and started making his way around the desk.

The time on a clock said 7:35 p.m. and Kevin realized the news was already halfway through and he had no idea where to go from there. He could hear a phone ringing at the security's desk.

He noticed that Sean was looking at him with a worried face, and he ignored him.

One thing he was certain of was that the country was about to know the truth, one way or the other.

The security from the car park burst through the door, gasping for air and informed his colleague that both men had come into the building without his permission. It was then that the officer belonging to the desk placed his focus on Kevin's face and attempted to reach for his firearm. Kevin had managed to pull out his firearm first and both guards threw up their hands, surrendering to him.

"I need to see Ms. Smith," Kevin said and without hesitation the officer from the desk gave him directions to the newsroom which was on the first floor.

Sean agreed to keep an eye on the two officers and after they had locked up the building, Kevin made his way upstairs as directed.

There wasn't anyone on the first floor and the newsroom was behind a large wooden door at the end of the corridor. Kevin continued walking and stopped when he saw the large logo on the door and realized that he had made it.

As he walked closer to the door he felt as though his mind had gone into a daze and he started getting flashes of everything that he'd been through.

He saw the look on Shantel's face as he walked out of the house and entered the car. He remembered being kicked up on the ground moments before the shootout. He saw himself running through the bushes as Biggs and his boys were shooting after him, and from there he remembered diving through the window and then driving away as the officers shot at him. His body twitched as he felt the loud explosion that took Wendell's life, and then he saw himself lying face down on the ground with bullet holes in his body. Seeing himself lying on the ground like that brought him back to reality. His body was cold, and his hands were wet and shaking.

He reached for the door and before pushing it open he got a clear image of Shantel with the baby in her hand. There was a proud look on her face and he knew she was counting on him to reunite with them no matter the circumstances. He whispered that he loved her and pushed the door open and entered the room.

There was a man standing on the inside of the door with a microphone attached to his headset. He was monitoring the two camera men who were both standing in another room that was separated by a wall with a glass window like those in interrogation rooms.

Inside that room he could see a large map and a man was telling the country what to expect from the weather the following day. The man looked at Kevin and paused for a second, causing the man with the headset to turn and notice that there was a stranger in the room.

Kevin shifted out of the weather man's view and pulled the firearm and pointed it at the man with the headset, demanding his cooperation. The man's stare was an obvious indication that he was fearful of losing his life. He stood there looking at Kevin as if he'd seen a ghost. Kevin indicated with his hand and the man pulled off his headset and dropped it on the ground.

Another door opened within the room and Ms. Smith walked out. She too looked surprised and immediately threw her hands up, surrendering to him.

"Okay… Just take whatever you want," the man said in a nervous voice. Kevin was clueless until he realized that they had no idea who he was or what was taking place. Ms. Smith's eyes were closed, and she was breathing heavily and mumbling something to herself, probably praying to get out of the situation alive.

"No, stop. This is not a robbery." Kevin said and stepped back further. Ms. Smith gradually opened her eyes. Her chin was down.

"Put down allyuh hands." Their hands went down hesitantly.

"Okay, no problem, everything cool," the man continued saying. "Just take whatever you want and you could go. We eh see nothing."

"No, is nothing like that. I is Kevin Jones, the person the police looking for."

Ms. Smith lifted her head and began studying his face. Her body was as stiff as a manikin's.

"Ms. Smith. Corporal Gibson send me by you." She looked as though she was trying to understand. "Concerning the video with the police and the drug house."

The man was looking at both of them, confused as to what was going on.

"Or, yes…yes, Gibson. I remember." She kept her hands away from her body, showing that she meant no harm. "Mister Gibson already talk to me concerning that. You have the memory card?"

"Yeah." At that instant Kevin wasn't sure whether he should feel relieved or not. He stuck his hand into his pocket and pulled out the memory card.

He noticed that the man had finished explaining the weather forecast, and everyone in that room was starting to move around. It was already eight o'clock.

She realized that he was becoming worried.

"Listen," she started saying. "Don't worry about them. Mister Gibson already tell me what it have on the memory card. All the cameras off. Let me go and explain what going on, and we would take a look at the memory card and broadcast it after, okay?"

Kevin was starting to feel a lot better. "When you broadcasting it? Tonight?"

"Yes. As soon as we see enough we would announce that we have breaking news, and I would personally broadcast it." She gave him her word. Whether her word meant anything, he'd soon find out.

"Yeah," He thought about it and slowly nodded.

"Okay."

The man seemed relaxed now.

"Okay. I would just take this." She stretched out her hand and he handed the memory card to her. "Just follow me and I would go inside and have a word with everybody." She turned, and they led Kevin to the main room with the news stand and all the camera equipment. Kevin stood at the door with the gun and everyone in the room seemed confused and worried.

Ms. Smith told them that everything was going to be okay before walking across the room and speaking to a man in a suit. They spoke for a few minutes and then she stuck the memory card into a computer next to him. As they viewed the footage, everyone moved closer to them and looked on. Some of them whispered to her and Kevin looked on as she explained the situation to them. On seeing and hearing the way they all protested against the officers actions, Kevin felt confident that everything would work out.

It had taken them about fifteen minutes of fast-forwarding and playing the video before they were satisfied with what they saw. When the video was stopped, Ms. Smith came to Kevin and asked him a few questions about what he had experienced and when she was finished he was left waiting again.

He kept his fingers crossed and his heart began racing with anxiety when he saw her make her way to the set and took her seat and waited for the cameras to come back on. Everyone started moving around again and then they'd signaled that she would be going live in five. When she was on she did as she'd promised and made the announcement that there was breaking news and a new twist in the Kevin Jones story.

She made a great introduction and then criticized the law enforcement authority before showing selected parts of the footage.

They were sure to put up their parental discretion declaimer and blur out anything that was not suitable for viewers. She also mentioned that Kevin had been threatened to accept responsibility for crimes he did not commit.

After she'd given her closing statement and the cameras were off she made a copy of the memory card before returning it to Kevin. He thanked her and her colleagues for everything that they've done, and she wished him all the best in the future.

One of the camera men mentioned that the police were downstairs and that was when he turned to leave.

As Kevin slowly made his way down he was thinking about the possible outcome of the situation, and as he turned to the last flight of stairs he could see the blue lights flashing against the wall. As much as he wasn't ready to face his fate he had no choice but to continue walking.

He stopped and took a deep breath before making the final step into the dazzling light.

He squinted and put his hands to his face in an attempt to limit the light. When his eyes adjusted he noticed that the car park was filled with police and soldiers and a lot of news personnel were also amongst them. They were already taking photos. Behind them Kevin could see random persons gathering to get a glimpse of what was about to take place.

Kevin walked closer to Sean who had already made his way around the counter when he noticed him.

The first thing Kevin noticed was the security officer's firearm bulging on Sean's waist right where it was concealed beneath his clothes. Then he realized that both of the officers were now standing behind the glass door.

"What you planning to do?" Sean said to him in a low panicking voice as if anyone outside could possibly hear what they were saying.

"You hear anything about Steve?"

Sean shook his head with a saddened face. Kevin couldn't stop thinking about the worst, but with everything that had happened, he hoped that Steve was okay.

He looked outside and studied the situation while he thought about Sean's question. He then shook his head and told Sean that he wasn't sure.

Sean looked disappointed and in his frustration he turned and made his way back to the chair behind the desk and like a stubborn child he sank himself into it.

Kevin thought he'd worked out everything, but he hadn't planned for it to turn out the way it did. He was grateful that he had accomplished what he had set out to do, but he was starting to realize that there was a possibility that things could still to go downhill.

As he stood there trying to work out another plan he noticed a group of officers dressed in riot gear began assembling in front of the glass door. During that moment persons from the newsroom started making their way downstairs and when they noticed that Kevin was still in the building they occupied a corner of the lobby. Kevin studied their frightened faces and realized the officers could use the opportunity to make it look like a hostage rescue situation. That was something he'd have to avoid in order to continue showing that he was innocent.

He shared his focus between Sean and the persons from the newsroom and it was then that he had willingly accepted the fact that the officers didn't want anyone else besides him. Lucky for them he wasn't willing to jeopardize anyone's safety either.

While looking at Sean their eyes met, and after they held their stare for a while Sean got up as if he knew just what Kevin was thinking and he made his way around the desk and came over to him.

"You not planning to do what I thinking, right?" Sean said. Kevin looked at him and shook his head and told him there wasn't any other way.

Sean started laughing in a hysterical way and then locked his hands behind his neck and started pacing back and forth as if that was the only way he could think. He looked at Kevin.

"You can't be serious, right? After all this you just going to walk out there?"

Kevin didn't answer. He had already made up his mind.

"What about if they shoot you down?"

He looked at the crowd and reminded himself that there were too many persons with cameras. Nevertheless, he knew if there was a possibility of him being shot it would be on his way to the station. And even during that time, more than likely, reporters would still be trailing behind.

He remembered that he still had the firearm on him and he signaled Sean to follow him and they started walking towards the counter.

When they were hidden behind the counter he removed his firearm, unloaded it and rested it on the lower surface. He watched Sean hesitantly do the same. When they were finished they wished each other good luck and headed for the glass doors with their hands above their heads in a surrender position.

They waited at the door for a moment and without a hint one of the men from the newsroom ran across, opened the door and ran back over to his colleagues.

The blue lights seemed brighter and Kevin started squinting his eyes again, and although he could hear a lot of talking coming from within the crowd the flashing of the cameras was sounding very clear.

The officers who were dressed in the riot gear were the first ones outside the door and as the majority of officers kept their firearms pointed at them, two of the officers came and placed handcuffs on their hands and began moving them through the crowd and towards an awaiting police vehicle.

There were officers on both side of them separating the crowd and when Kevin lifted his head in the direction of the awaiting vehicle he saw the chief standing there, holding the door open.

Kevin felt his heart skipped a beat and he almost choked on his breath. As he attempted to clear his throat he could feel his body becoming weak and he stumbled but the officer had managed to keep him on his feet.

He could feel the officer piercing his fingers into his

arm as they continued walking towards the vehicle.

When Kevin was face to face with the chief, he was pushed into the vehicle by the officer and the chief slammed the door shut.

Inside the vehicle was dark and empty but Kevin managed to get on to his knees and he made his way over to a small vent to the back of the vehicle that was protected by iron bars.

Outside, he could see Sean being led into another police vehicle. Sean was shouting and cursing at the officers as they tried to get him into the vehicle. At one point more officers joined in and Sean continued kicking and throwing around his body. The officers had formed a wall around him, blocking him from the public's view and two officers started beating him with their batons. It was only then that he'd stop resisting and they'd finally got him into the vehicle and closed the door.

Kevin turned and carefully got his body in a sitting position. He shook his head in pity, since he knew resisting wouldn't have made a difference. He'd already done his part and was prepared to wait for the results.

The vehicle started moving and he shifted his body in a more settled position to withstand the rough ride.

He felt the vehicle exit the parking lot and made a sharp right turn and at that immediate moment he heard the deafening sound of a siren that lasted for only a few seconds. The siren brought the vehicle to a brief stop and Kevin got on his knees and went to the vent again.

He could only see the vehicle behind in which Sean was being held and three additional vehicles that were all part of the convoy. The commotion was to the front but there was no way for him to know what was actually taking place.

Kevin remained at the vent and after a few minutes had passed he saw three men dressed in black suits appeared and walk towards the vehicles and instructed the officers to come out.

The men in the suits said something to the officers and they'd all gone out of sight.

Kevin was anxious to know what was going on and after a short wait he heard a noise at the door and then it slid open. He kept his eyes in the direction and saw a tall dark-skinned man in a black suit standing in the darkness with a machine gun hanging across his chest. The man instructed Kevin to get out of the vehicle and Kevin went without hesitating.

On his way out, Kevin noticed several black cars with blue blinking lights on both sides of the dashboard. He looked over his shoulder and saw that the Police Commissioner was being interviewed by a group of reporters.

The man who had called him gently removed the handcuffs from where it was behind his back and placed it to the front instead. Kevin was amazed by the way he was being treated in such a short time.

The man had then put him into one of the vehicles and when he looked to his side he saw Sean sitting next to him. They both looked at each other in silence and Kevin was glad to know that they were in good hands.

Kevin noticed several reporters running towards the front of the vehicle and when he looked in the direction he saw the chief and six other officers being led into the back of two of the vehicles.

He saw the reporters being stopped and turned away by a group of officers who had quickly formed a barrier in front of both vehicles.

Almost forty-five minutes had gone by before the commissioner had walked away from the reporters and entered one of the vehicles and only then they were given the clearance to drive away.

Kevin studied Sean's quiet expression for a minute and then he placed his head on the seat in front of him and began thinking of what it would be like when he was actually free. He had no doubt that he'd have to serve some time and he was prepared for it.

One thing he was proud of was the fact that he had finally corrected his mistakes and that was most important to him.

He eventually sat upright and looked out the window as they sped pass the buildings and within a short time he began daydreaming of the smile on Shantel and his baby girl's face as he walked over to them for the first time after his release.

He smiled and made a promise to himself that when that day came he would be ready to dedicate all his time and effort to both of them. It was a promise he was willing to keep.

It was two o'clock in the afternoon and Kevin was sitting in the arrival area of the airport. He was holding a large Disney character gift bag in his hand as he waited anxiously for Shantel to clear the immigration officers and come through the automatic doors. Persons had already started making their way through and that was making him more nervous.

This would be the first time he'd be seeing his daughter after serving a three-year-long sentence. He also had a pending matter against the State. If won, he could be awarded up to $450,000 for damages.

During his sentence, he would use inmates' phones to communicate with Shantel who was staying at a family's home in Miami with their daughter. She would also visit him on a regular basis whenever she returned to Trinidad. She would come alone since Kevin refused for his daughter to see him under such conditions. It was a difficult and emotional sacrifice, but he'd managed to survive through everything.

Kevin saw the doors open and stood up when he saw Shantel and his daughter walk through dragging their bags behind.

Shantel had noticed him and with a bright smile she made her way over to him and he stood and kept her in a warm hug for a while. His daughter was hiding behind Shantel. When Kevin had loosened his grip, he went down to his knees and presented his baby girl with her birthday present. She was hesitant at first, but after Shantel told her who he was, she took it and felt more comfortable being in his presence.

After a few minutes in each other's company, he reminded her of their phone calls and the promises he had made and she'd finally accepted his hug. He held on to her with emotions beyond his expectations.

He arranged the bags and they left the airport to enjoy the reunion they had dreamt of.